The Village Choir Killer

ALSO BY FRANCES LLOYD

DETECTIVE INSPECTOR JACK DAWES
Book 1: The Greek Island Killer
Book 2: The Bluebell Killer
Book 3: The Shetland Island Killer
Book 4: The Gallows Green Killer
Book 5: The Moon Killer
Book 6: The Kings Market Killer
Book 7: The Demon Killer
Book 8: The Vale Vineyard Killer
Book 9: The Brightsea Spa Killer
Book 10: The Kings Copse Killer
Book 11: The Eden Park Killer
Book 12: The Coat of Arms Killer
Book 13: The Village Choir Killer

THE VILLAGE CHOIR KILLER

FRANCES LLOYD

DI Jack Dawes Murder Mystery Book 13

Joffe Books, London
www.joffebooks.com

First published in Great Britain in 2025

© Frances Lloyd 2025

This book is a work of fiction. Names, characters, businesses, organizations, places and events are either the product of the author's imagination or are used fictitiously. Any resemblance to actual persons, living or dead, events or locales is entirely coincidental. The spelling used is British English except where fidelity to the author's rendering of accent or dialect supersedes this. The right of Frances Lloyd to be identified as author of this work has been asserted in accordance with the Copyright, Designs and Patents Act 1988.

No part of this book may be used or reproduced in any manner for the purpose of training artificial intelligence technologies or systems. In accordance with Article 4(3) of the Digital Single Market Directive 2019/790, Joffe Books expressly reserves this work from the text and data mining exception.

Cover art by Dee Dee Book Covers

ISBN: 978-1-80573-152-8

PROLOGUE

Community choirs bring together people of all ages, united through song and a shared purpose. People have various motives for joining. Some want to try something out of the ordinary, to explore a new skill. Others seek to find company and a sense of belonging. By making their personal contribution to a bigger, more cohesive sound, they feel valued and gain a sense of well-being. But in a matter of weeks, the Richington Community Choir turned into something far different from the enjoyable experience for which it was set up — something much less wholesome. It became an opportunity for blackmail, deception and — murder.

Bryn Thomas, the choirmaster — or Maestro, as he preferred to be called — had his own reasons for leaving the male voice choir in Wales and starting a new ensemble in the affluent, rapidly expanding town of Kings Richington. Felicity, his wife, amanuensis and general dogsbody, trotted dutifully in his wake, organizing practice sessions, booking performances and managing the choir's website. She also provided tea and her infamous rock buns for the intervals.

But the choir didn't just exist as a feel-good experience for its members. Many local charities benefited from the money raised from their live performances, which took place in locations as diverse as fish markets, department stores and car boot sales — anywhere that people congregated in large, appreciative numbers. Here, the singers performed a popular mix of folk, operatic and musical theatre songs, even sea shanties, much to the Maestro's disdain. He saw himself as an artistic master — even a genius — with an enormous amount of skill and talent. He believed he was wasted on the dim-witted Richington plebs who, he had discovered, couldn't tell a crotchet from a quaver.

It was true the choir members came from a wide range of backgrounds and occupations: Geoff, a tenor, was a used-car salesman. Charlie, a rare basso-profundo, was a butcher. Jim, a baritone, ran the local pub and Roxy, a mezzo-soprano, owned a shop selling lurid lingerie and dubious adult toys. Their motivations for joining were as varied as their occupations: Elizabeth, a contralto and a Doctor of Theology, was chasing votes in the hope of becoming the next mayor. Charlie saw it as an opportunity to get close to young women in a way that in any other setting would have been deemed highly inappropriate. Luke, a young counter-tenor who took the lead in songs requiring an unusually high range for a male singer, had been separated from his family at birth. For him, the choir was a welcome place to connect and find the friendship that the other singers offered. The ages of the choristers ranged from eighty-four-year-old widow Violet Dibble to seventeen-year-old Ellie, a gifted soprano, who sang to help control the symptoms of her asthma.

But within this eclectic and superficially harmless ensemble, there lurked the threat of evil. Behind the scenes, the dynamics between the members were far less innocent than they appeared. These were people whose paths would probably never have crossed, let alone formed any kind of symbiotic relationship, had it not been for the choir. As for the impact on their nearest and dearest, Charlie Snell's wife and Dr Amory's husband would have reported very different views.

The opening post on the Community Choir's blog claimed that singing could be life-changing, but for one member at least, it was a death sentence.

CHAPTER ONE

The morning sunlight was just beginning to filter through the trees as Dr Elizabeth Amory ran purposefully along the forest path. She was training for a half marathon, so she knew it was important to keep track of her pace. Her target was to cover ten kilometres in an hour. With that in mind, it had taken only a second to glance down at her smartwatch, but in that second of distraction, she lost her rhythm and stumbled over what she thought was a fallen oak branch. She pitched forward onto her knees.

'Bugger!' She could swear with impunity out here in the forest, without damaging her carefully honed reputation for decency and virtue. Hers was a life of good works and commitment to the Kings Richington community, which she had nurtured over a number of years. It was the widespread acclaim which she hoped would propel her into the role of mayor, the highest-ranking official in municipal government.

While she was fumbling about, looking for her water bottle, she realized that it wasn't a branch she'd tripped over — it was a man's leg. He was lying face down in the decaying vegetation that formed the forest litter with an ugly slash of dried blood across the back of his head. She cursed again, more forcefully this time, then reached out to feel his neck for a pulse. He was stiff and cold — beyond help. Scrambling to her feet, she pulled out her phone and punched in the emergency number.

* * *

'They've found a body in Richington Forest, guv.' Detective Sergeant Mike 'Bugsy' Malone was short, overweight and prone to wearing his suits long after the trousers had reached the age of retirement. He put down the phone and shouted across the incident room to his boss. 'A lady jogger called it in and Norman has sent uniforms to secure the scene. Big Ron and her SOCOs are already there.' The pathologist, Dr Veronica Hardacre, was known affectionately, albeit covertly, as Big Ron on account of her powerful frame and even more powerful personality. She was brusque, brilliant and took no prisoners when it came to senior detectives demanding immediate answers to their questions before she was prepared to give them.

As usual, Sergeant Norman Parsloe had been on the desk when the call came through. There were young coppers at the station who reckoned Sergeant Parsloe had been on the desk when the Bow Street Runners were pounding the beat. They also knew that his knowledge of the area and the villains who infested it was second to none and had often provided the vital catalyst to an arrest. If you wanted to know the criminal history of any repeat offender, you asked Sergeant Parsloe.

Detective Inspector Jack Dawes, head of the Kings Richington Murder Investigation Team, drained the last of his coffee and reached for his coat. A wiry six foot three, he was sartorially the yang to Malone's yin. Tall, angular and with striking, if crooked, features, Jack was always smart with highly polished shoes and a crisp white shirt under a perfectly pressed suit. Bugsy was the short, rotund opposite, more often than not displaying the evidence of a fried breakfast down his tie. But together, they made up a harmonious, complementary partnership that demonstrated the success of contradictions within the same police environment.

Jack became aware of amused mutterings around the room at the mention of a jogger. The team knew his views on the ubiquitous joggers and dog walkers who always seemed to be the first to discover murder victims, especially early in the morning. 'Contrary to popular belief,' he announced, 'I don't have a problem with joggers. I just wish they'd stick to sprinting about the park in their underwear, instead of combing the countryside, tripping over corpses and trampling all over murder scenes.'

'I doubt if this lady was jogging in her underwear,' observed Bugsy. 'According to Norman, who knows everything about everybody around here, she's a pillar of the Kings Richington community.' Bugsy looked at the notes he'd scribbled down during the phone call. 'Her name's Dr Elizabeth Amory and she lives at Richington Court — that swanky house on the outskirts of town. She's Chair of the Town Council, runs Heritage Open Days and does regular stints at the Community Day Centre — and that's just in her spare time. She's pretty hot on climate change, too, apparently.'

'I'm not sure "hot" is the right word, Sarge,' remarked Detective Constable Gemma Fox. Intelligent, with a law degree and immaculately styled blonde hair, Gemma was the pragmatic one of the team. 'I think "hot" is what we're all trying to avoid.'

'Unless you're trudging through the freezing rain doing door-to-door enquiries.' Detective Constable Aled Williams, muscular and fit, spoke from bitter experience as a constable in uniform before he'd joined MIT.

'Do we have a name for the victim?' asked Jack.

'Not yet, guv, just that it's a bloke. Forensic officers are still going through his pockets.'

'OK. Let's go, Bugsy.'

* * *

They found Dr Amory sitting on a log in a forest clearing. As Bugsy had predicted, she wasn't in her 'underwear'; she was in full designer sports gear, including a pair of running shoes that he reckoned would see off a month's salary. Her short dark hair was covered by a swoosh cap and she wore thermal running gloves and a hip pack. Bugsy was reminded of the expression 'all the gear — no idea', but he doubted that applied here. This lady meant business. She looked irritated by what she'd found but not unduly traumatized. When Jack and Bugsy showed her their warrant cards, she glanced at them briefly and nodded.

'Thank you for waiting, Dr Amory.' Jack held out a hand, which she grasped firmly, after pulling off one of her gloves. He guessed her to be around forty, but she was lithe and fit so could easily have been younger, and as his wife was always telling him, he was hopeless at guessing women's ages. 'Can you tell us what time you found the body?'

She glanced at her watch and pressed a few buttons on the side. 'It would have been about seven fifteen. I'd just finished my first five kilometres when I fell over his legs.'

'You didn't touch anything?' asked Malone.

'Only his neck to see if he had a pulse — he didn't. And rigor mortis was well advanced. There was nothing I could do.' She pulled out a water bottle and took a couple of good swigs.

'As a doctor, I suppose you would have recognized the signs,' assumed Jack.

She shook her head. 'I'm not a medical doctor, Inspector. I'm a Doctor of Theology. I look after people's souls, not their bodies — although some would argue that you can't have one without the other.' She gestured to where the pathologist and the SOCOs were grouped around the corpse. 'Mind you, I think it might be too late to save Charlie's soul.'

Jack and Bugsy exchanged surprised glances. 'Did you know the deceased, Madam?' asked Bugsy.

'Oh yes. It's Charlie Snell. I recognized him straight away from that absurd ponytail he insisted on wearing and the disgusting scruffy beard that always looked suspiciously like it contained the remains of his last meal. His death hasn't increased his charm at all. He owns the butcher's in the high street — Charlie's Chop Shop. Ghastly name, don't you think?'

'Did you buy your meat there?' asked Jack.

'Absolutely not. My husband, Julian, and I are vegans. I don't even like walking past the shop. It's the smell, you see. Blood and raw flesh.' She shuddered.

'Surely you don't think Mr Snell's soul is in peril because he's a butcher?' Jack knew feelings ran high over such beliefs, but all the same, he imagined a Doctor of Theology would be rather more forgiving.

She gave him a disdainful look. 'No, of course not. Although I daresay our Lord would prefer it if we didn't go around killing His creatures and eating them. No, it was Mr Snell's other proclivities that I, and several other folk, objected to.'

'And what might those have been, Madam?' asked Bugsy.

'He was an all-round nasty piece of work, Sergeant,' she said bluntly, 'and he was a groper. Never missed a chance to put his hands somewhere inappropriate. And despite being our only basso-profundo, he usually managed to creep around behind the young sopranos. Well, you can imagine . . .'

'I'm sorry, Doctor, but you've lost me.' Bugsy was confused. 'I thought you said the deceased was a butcher.'

She tutted impatiently as if explaining to a particularly difficult child. 'He was, but he was also a member of the Richington Community Choir — as am I. Our paths would never have crossed otherwise, would they? Do keep up, Sergeant. Of course, I don't really have time for the choir, but I sing contralto. It's quite rare. It's estimated that only about two per cent of the female population have a contralto range, so I feel obliged to contribute when I can.'

'Is there a Mrs Snell?' asked Jack, conscious that next of kin should be informed as a priority.

'Yes, I think her name's Delphine or Darleen — anyway, it's something with "een" on the end. She's a large lady, booming voice. She isn't in the choir, though. She comes to fetch him on practice nights to make sure he doesn't wander off, if you get my drift.' She stood up. 'Look, can I go now? I'm stiffening up sitting on this log and I've another 5k to run before breakfast.'

Jack stood up. 'Yes, of course, Doctor. Thank you for your help. We'll be in touch later for a formal statement.'

'Well, you know where I am if you want me. My address is Richington Court; it's the only halfway decent house in town — detached, pseudo-Tudor on the outskirts. You can't miss it.' She clicked her watch a few times and loped off through the trees, leaving the police officers somewhat bemused.

'Well, what do you make of that, guv?' asked Bugsy.

'Quite useful, I'd say, as initial murder enquiries go. We already know the identity of the deceased, where he was killed and when the body was found — now, we just need to know time and cause of death, who did it and why, and we've cracked it.'

'I can help with some of that.' Dr Hardacre, the pathologist, had finished her examination and came striding across to explain. 'Morning, Inspector Dawes, Sergeant Malone.' She pulled off the hood of her white protective suit, revealing spiky black hair and eyebrows and the hint of a moustache. 'He died where he fell, I'd guess around nine to eleven hours ago. The most obvious cause of death was blunt force trauma. Somebody bashed the poor devil over the back of the head with this . . .' She held up a large evidence bag containing a sturdy branch from an oak tree, with dried blood on one end. 'No sign of a struggle and no other injuries — one clout did it. And there are only three sets of footprints around him in the mulch, the victim's, the killer's and, minimally, Dr Amory's running shoes. She had the good sense not to trample all over what she could see was a crime scene. We found another set of larger footprints approaching the perimeter of the clearing. It looks like somebody stood there for a few minutes and then walked away, but they might not be directly connected to the crime. You already know from Dr

Amory who he is, but as for who did it and why — that, as always, is your job, Inspector, but I can tell you that it wasn't robbery. His wallet contained a hundred pounds, he had the latest mobile phone, and he's wearing a heavy gold bracelet on one wrist and a very decent watch on the other. I'll give you a more comprehensive report after the post-mortem. Shall we say two thirty?' She stomped back to the forensics van where the mortuary men were poised to take away the body.

There being nothing more to examine, the two detectives made their way back to the car. 'I know your favourite theory, Sergeant, is that the person who found the body is usually the murderer . . .' began Jack.

'Fair dos, guv, I've even been right a couple of times,' protested Bugsy, fishing in his pocket for the emergency sausage roll he always kept there.

'. . . but I think you'll agree, it's unlikely in this case,' finished Jack. 'As far as a motive is concerned, I doubt whether the virtuous Dr Amory would be driven to murder simply because Snell owned a shop selling dead animals and couldn't keep his hands to himself.'

'Of course,' added Bugsy, chewing, 'my other favourite theory is that the murderer is either the victim's spouse or a business partner and there's money at the back of it.'

Jack paused, his hands resting on the wheel. 'Has this job made us cynical, d'you think?'

'No, guv. It's just that common sense dictates you try the most obvious lines of enquiry first and if they don't provide the solution, you dig into the more obscure stuff.'

'OK, so first off, we'll go and break the news to the bereaved widow. We'll pick up DC Fox on the way to deal with the tea and tissues.'

* * *

Mrs Snell's first name was, in fact, Doreen. She lived with Charlie in a flat over the butcher's shop which they allegedly ran together, but it was obvious that she did most of the work. Fortunately, the shop was empty of customers when Jack, Bugsy and Gemma pushed open the door. Doreen Snell was behind the counter, hair imprisoned in a net and hacking a loin of pork into chops with a formidable cleaver. She was a well-built woman, as Dr Amory had described, and wore a white overall with bloodstains down the front. She glanced up briefly as they approached. 'What can I get you, gentlemen, and Madam? The fillet steak is particularly good today.'

'Mrs Snell?' enquired Jack, holding out his warrant card. 'We're police officers. Might we have a word, please? It's about your husband.'

She sighed wearily. 'OK, what's the lazy, two-timing drunk done this time?' By way of emphasis, she brought the cleaver down with a whack that made Bugsy wince.

'Perhaps we could have a chat somewhere more private?' suggested Jack.

She baulked at this. 'Certainly not! In case you hadn't noticed, this is a butcher's shop and I rely on selling meat to customers to make a living. I don't have time to chat. Just tell me which nick you're holding him in and I'll come and fetch him after I've closed up.'

Bugsy had already turned the sign on the door to 'Closed'. 'I'm afraid it's bad news, Mrs Snell.'

She became aware then of their sombre faces and put down the meat cleaver. 'All right, you'd better come up.'

They followed her upstairs into the drawing room and Gemma went into the tiny kitchen to put on the kettle. In her relatively short experience of what were known as 'death calls', a cup of tea was always required, often accompanied by a generous shot of whisky or brandy, depending on availability and the preference of the bereaved. She didn't have a husband and wasn't planning on one, so she wondered what it must feel like to be told suddenly that the man you had been married to was dead.

Whatever Jack was expecting when he told Doreen Snell the news, it wasn't the long, stony silence.

Eventually she asked, 'How did he die?'

'I'm afraid he was murdered. His body was discovered in Richington Forest early this morning. He'd been hit over the head.' Jack waited in silence while she slowly assimilated this. He was unable to guess from her expression what was going on in her head. 'When did you last see your husband, Mrs Snell?'

She had to think about it. 'It would have been yesterday evening, when he left for choir practice.'

'Didn't you wonder where he was when he didn't come home?' asked Bugsy.

She frowned. 'You didn't know my husband, Sergeant, otherwise you wouldn't have asked that question. If I'm not there to drag him home by the scruff of the neck as soon as choir practice is over, he's off after anything in skirts, mostly that flashy piece from the knicker shop down the road. Last night, I was late because there was a problem with one of the freezers and it took me a while to fix it. When I got to the church hall, he'd already left.'

'So did you go and look for him?' asked Bugsy.

She bridled. 'I wouldn't lower myself. I thought I'd just wait for him to come creeping in, then go down and give him a good hiding. But I fell asleep, and this morning, when he still hadn't come home, I opened up the shop and got on with earning a living. He always came home eventually, no matter whose bed he'd slept in.' She sniffed. 'But he isn't going to this time, is he?'

Gemma listened to her, confused by Doreen's illogical feelings for her husband and baffled by what this woman, and scores like her, were prepared to put up with from miserable, philandering excuses for partners rather than be alone. In her opinion, it wasn't much of a life and it reinforced her conviction never to marry. What was wrong with the single life, anyway?

'Did Mr Snell have any enemies, as far as you know?' Bugsy asked gently.

She laughed without humour. 'Never mind *any* enemies, Sergeant, he had *only* enemies. He certainly wasn't what you'd call popular. Sometimes I think he went out of his way to be unpleasant. Most people would cross the road to avoid him, especially young women. But I can't think of anyone who disliked him enough to kill him.'

'Is there someone you'd like us to contact to come and be with you, Mrs Snell?' asked Jack.

'Only my son, Bradley. He's studying at Leicester University. He'll have to be told, although he never got on with his father, even when he was little, so I doubt he'll shed many tears.'

'We can arrange for your son to be brought home, Mrs Snell,' suggested Gemma.

'Oh no, please, you mustn't do that!' Doreen nearly spilled her tea in her haste to prevent such a thing happening. 'He worked so hard to get into uni and he takes his finals this year. I shouldn't want to upset his studies.'

'Not even to pay his last respects to his father?' Gemma was shocked.

'Especially not for that. You see, his father thought going to university was a waste of four years when he should be helping out in the shop. Bradley was never going to do that. He didn't want to be a butcher; he's studying to be an aerospace engineer. They had violent arguments about it.'

'When you say "violent", did these arguments ever become physical?' Jack wondered to what extent Charlie Snell would go to try to keep a promising son as cheap labour in a second-rate butcher's shop. He'd obviously regarded his wife as such.

'Yes, they fought. At least, they did until the last time Bradley came home. Charlie tried to bully him into giving up his education and started to slap him and push him around, like he did when he was a kiddie. Only these days, Bradley's six foot three of solid muscle and he'd had enough. He punched his father hard on the jaw. It was only the one punch, but Charlie went down with such a wallop he was too dazed to stand up. Bradley dragged him to his feet and said, "If you lay a finger on me ever again, I'll kill you."' She realized the implication of what she'd said and immediately retracted. 'He didn't mean it, of course. You mustn't think that.'

'Was Charlie ever violent to you, Mrs Snell?' asked Bugsy.

Her response was scathing. 'He wouldn't have dared. You've seen the size of him — ten stone dripping wet. If he'd ever hit me, I'd have flattened him and he knew it.'

They left Doreen, insisting that she was perfectly fine and intended to reopen the shop and carry on working. She agreed to come to the mortuary and make a formal identification, but there was little doubt that it was Charlie Snell's worthless life of flagrant disregard for anyone but himself that was at an end and few, if anyone, would mourn his passing. But even so, DI Dawes and his MIT had to solve his murder and that meant finding someone with the means, opportunity and a strong enough motive to want him dead.

CHAPTER TWO

The Murder Investigation Team was one of the specialized homicide squads of the London Metropolitan Police Service and formed part of Scotland Yard's Serious Crime Group. The Commands were split geographically, with each unit led by a Detective Chief Superintendent — in the case of Kings Richington this was George Garwood. But for him, this was only a stepping stone. Garwood was a careers man, determined to rise to the top of his profession, maybe even retire with a knighthood. To this end, he relied on DI Dawes to keep turning in a clear-up rate that consistently put Kings Richington at the top of the table.

In the MIT incident room, Jack was sitting at his desk jotting down his thoughts on a notepad. Although Clive, the team's digital forensic specialist, had set up an excellent user-friendly programme on his computer which served the same purpose, somehow his brain didn't produce the same results as when he actually wrote something down on paper with a pen. He guessed it was an age thing.

Clive had his heavy black-framed glasses perched on his nose and was searching social media for any information about the Richington Community Choir, since that was where the deceased was last seen alive. In the event, there was quite a lot.

'What have you got, Clive?' Bugsy swallowed the last of his jumbo blackcurrant pie from the canteen and brushed sticky pastry from the front of his jacket. It had been some hours since his wife, Iris, had put a full English breakfast in front of him and he felt his brain didn't work efficiently if the gaps between sustenance were too long. And despite medical advice to the contrary, he firmly believed himself to be pastry-dependent, which meant keeping a cache of sausage rolls and fruit pies in his desk drawer for whenever he felt the onset of withdrawal symptoms.

'The choir has its own blog, Sarge,' reported Clive. 'This is their introductory post.' Clive read it aloud for the whole team to hear.

> *We are a small, friendly community choir (around twenty, including Bryn Thomas, our Maestro) with members from Kings Richington and surrounding villages. We meet every Wednesday night in the church hall or the room above the Richington Arms and practise in the Community Hall when available. We provide choral support to St Boniface Church on special occasions. New members are always welcome to audition.*

'And this one is their last post before Charlie Snell copped it,' added Clive.

> *Huge thanks to all our choir members who braved the stormy weather to sing at the Kings Richington Community Hub yesterday. We are continuing our busy week by singing folk songs at the Kings Richington Ladies Coffee and Crochet Club at 11 am tomorrow. All are welcome, including men. Refreshments provided.*

'There's a pic of the choir practising in the Community Hall, sir,' added Clive.

'What do they look like — as a choral society, I mean?' asked Jack.

'Er . . . well, put it this way, sir, you wouldn't mistake them for the King's College choristers, but they don't look like a bunch of murderers, either. When they're performing, they wear matching red tee-shirts and a kind of white sash with the name of the choir printed on it. The choirmaster seems to be wearing a long red frock with embroidery down the front.'

'I think you'll find it's called a robe.' Coming from Wales, DC Williams had had some experience in a choir, and thinking back to the burly choirmaster who played scrum half for Pontypool RFC, he didn't think he'd have appreciated it being called a frock.

'I'll enlarge the photo and print it out for the whiteboard.'

The team gathered around to look at what was, effectively, the last known picture of Charlie Snell before his unexpected if not wholly unpopular demise. Typically, the camera had caught him looking lasciviously down the cleavage of the voluptuous lady standing beside him, rather than paying attention to the choirmaster, like the others.

'Where do you want us to start, sir?' DC 'Chippy' Chippendale was relatively new to the MIT and very keen to make a good impression. He was polite, clean-cut, and looked about twelve years old.

Chippy came from a close-knit, wealthy family in New Zealand, the youngest of three brothers and two sisters. They all had creative careers and it had come as something of a surprise when their little brother announced that instead of playing the flute, as his mother had mapped out for him, he was going to join the police service in the UK. Nevertheless, they supported him totally and were delighted when he'd made the progression from police constable to detective. Only his mother was disapproving, vowing it wouldn't end well.

Jack was pondering. 'I think that despite Mrs Snell's possibly biased description of her husband as a lazy, drunken skirt-chaser, we need to find out more about his other habits to establish a credible motive for his murder. But from what Dr Amory told us, I don't think we'll be short of candidates, particularly amongst members of that choir. She seemed to regard them all with something akin to disdain. Of course, that doesn't mean they're all closet criminals, but we need to speak to the choirmaster, get a list and do background checks. Clive, who manages this blog-thing?'

'It's Mrs Felicity Thomas, the wife of Bryn Thomas. He's the choirmaster.'

'Right, we'll start with her.' Jack looked at the clock. 'But first, Sergeant Malone and I have to attend the post-mortem. It may give us more information.'

* * *

As usual, the cloying antiseptic smells of the cold, sterile examination room caught in Jack's throat and he had to resist the urge to retch. He swallowed hard a few times. 'Good afternoon, Dr Hardacre.'

The pathologist was her usual waspish self and barely looked up as he and Bugsy approached the table on which the late Charlie Snell was laid out. 'You're late. I've nearly finished.' She tweezered something unpleasant into a dish held by her assistant, Miss Catwater.

'Anything useful to tell us, Doc?' asked Bugsy innocently.

'I hope everything I tell you is useful, Sergeant, otherwise I'm wasting your time and my breath. I can confirm that this man died sometime between ten o'clock and midnight from a single blow to the head, fracturing his occipital bone. It was administered with considerable force using the branch from an oak tree. There were no discernible fingerprints on it and only the deceased's DNA.'

'The blow wasn't struck by a woman, then,' assumed Bugsy.

'I didn't say that,' snapped Dr Hardacre. 'You'd be surprised at the strength that even a slightly built woman can summon, given sufficient provocation. It would have been dark in the forest at that time and it was raining, so it was a surprisingly accurate blow — either that or a lucky one.'

'It seems we aren't short of folk with a motive,' observed Jack glumly. 'Nobody liked him, not even his wife and son.'

'If you're looking for motivation, Inspector, you could start with all the customers of that health hazard of a butcher's shop he ran.' She indicated Miss Catwater. 'Poor Marigold suffered a violent stomach upset after eating his sausages. Goodness only knows what he put in them.'

Miss Catwater nodded vigorously. 'I reported him to the food standards people.'

'Snell was underweight, smoked, drank too much and had an enlarged prostate,' finished Dr Hardacre. 'Not unusual in a man of his age.'

'So there's nothing seriously wrong with him apart from the fact that he's dead,' quipped Bugsy.

'I think I'd have noticed if he'd been alive, Sergeant,' she retorted. 'I'll let you have the full report in the morning.'

* * *

When Jack and Bugsy turned up on Felicity Thomas's somewhat grand doorstep, it seemed to Jack that she'd been expecting them, but he could have been mistaken. She was an unremarkable woman with a permanently worried expression, reminding Bugsy of a basset hound he'd once owned. The baggy beige cardigan and long brown skirt did her no favours and her hair was scraped back in a messy bun. News obviously travelled fast in the choral community because it was evident that she'd already heard about the death of Charlie Snell. She showed them into the drawing room of the spacious Edwardian house and motioned to them to sit down. A grand piano took up most of the room with piles of music scores on the top. Bugsy was surprised as he thought all music was produced electronically these days and stored on things his step-grandkids called 'playlists'.

'I wonder if we might ask you a few questions about Charlie Snell, Madam,' Jack began.

Mrs Thomas seemed distracted and muttered, almost to herself, 'This has been such a shock — a terrible shock. I suppose I shall have to include some kind of obituary in this week's newsletter, but I've no idea what to write. I mean, an obituary is supposed to extoll the virtues of the deceased, but Charlie didn't have any.'

'How well did you know Mr Snell?' asked Jack.

'What . . .?' She looked vaguely from one officer to the other as if she'd only just realized they were there. 'Er . . . hardly at all, really. Only that he was rude and offensive and nobody in the choir liked him.'

'Do you think you could let us have a list of the other choir members, please?'

'Yes, of course. I'll email it to you . . .'

The door flew open behind them. 'I'll deal with this, Felicity. You get on with writing my script for next week's concert.' Bryn Thomas suddenly emerged from another reception room and effectively dismissed his wife before turning his attention to the detectives. Tall and thin, he sported a multicoloured silk tunic and untidy shoulder-length hair, presumably in an attempt to look musically bohemian, but not quite pulling it off due to the brown corduroys and plimsolls. He waved his arms expansively when Jack and Bugsy stood up, proffering their warrants. 'Please sit, gentlemen. I imagine this is about Snell. Tiresome business. The man was a crook and a sex pest. The only good thing about him was his voice — he was a basso- profundo. It's the lowest male voice type with a range of around E2 to E4.'

The two coppers looked blank.

'In case you aren't aware, it manifests as a low, rich rumble with massive vocal weight.' He frowned. 'They're rare. I don't know where I shall find another to replace him.'

'What makes you say he was a crook, Mr Thomas?' asked Jack, who was more interested in Snell's conduct than his voice.

'Well, ask yourself, Inspector.' Bryn's Welsh accent became more marked as he expressed his contempt. 'Where do you suppose he got the money to spend on fast cars and loose women, while his poor wife slaved in that miserable little butcher's shop?'

'Where do *you* think he got it, sir?' Bugsy thought they might be getting closer to a motive for murder. If Charlie Snell had been a grasping villain as well as a groping basso-profundo, there could be any number of suspects.

Thomas shrugged. 'I shouldn't want to speculate, but the rumours have already started.'

'Can you give us some examples, sir?'

'Well, if you insist. For a start, there are suspicions he was drug dealing from his shop. I can't provide evidence, otherwise I should have reported him, but people were observed going in but not coming out with any meat. Violet Dibble has him down as a latter-day Blue Beard with a string of dead wives and Luke thinks he's a paedophile because of his unwanted attention to young girls like Ellie.'

'So what do you think happened to him, Mr Thomas?'

'Well, I'd say he'd been lurking in Richington Forest for nefarious reasons when someone with a grudge crept up and bashed him over the head. That doesn't happen to decent, clean-living folk, does it? And what exactly was he up to in the first place? My guess is that he made an enemy of one person too many and that person finally caught up with him.'

'Did he get on well with the other members of the choir?' probed Jack, remembering what Felicity Thomas had said about him being unpopular. While there was no reason yet to suspect that one of them might have killed Charlie, Jack had a hunch that the choir might be a good place to start.

Thomas was dismissive. 'The man didn't have any friends, and as for enemies, he distributed his venom fairly evenly. I doubt whether he disliked any particular person any more than the rest. My choir members are respectable people. They didn't approve of his behaviour, but they did appreciate the vocal contribution Snell made to the choir, as did I. Otherwise, I should never have had anything to do with the man.'

Jack and Bugsy continued to question Bryn Thomas but didn't learn much more of any value except a growing conviction that this choir and its Maestro would need closer investigation. 'Just one more thing, Mr Thomas. Would you mind telling us where you were last night between the hours of ten and midnight?' Jack watched his face for any reaction.

He answered without hesitation. 'Choir practice finished at ten and after that, I was at home in bed with my wife, Inspector.'

'And she will confirm that, will she, sir?'

'Yes, of course. What are you inferring?'

'Nothing at all. It's just a routine question. It's normal procedure in a murder case to check where people were. We'll be in touch.'

Bryn watched them get into their car and drive away, then he went back inside. Felicity was standing behind the kitchen door where she'd been throughout Bryn's interview with the police. He scowled at her irritably. 'Why are you skulking behind the door? I suppose you listened in to every word?'

'Yes, I did, Bryn, and you lied. After we got home from choir practice, you went out again and you didn't get home until gone midnight. Where did you go?'

'If it's any of your business, I went for a walk to clear my head.' He flicked back his hair theatrically. 'That last folk song was particularly taxing.'

'So why didn't you tell the police that?'

'Because it's none of their business, that's why! And while we're on the subject of lying, you went out again, too, didn't you? I saw your coat on the hall stand and it was soaking wet from the rain. Where did you go?'

'Why are you even interested, Bryn?' she ventured. 'Do you think I was meeting my lover?'

He snorted with derision. 'A lover? You? Don't be ridiculous! Look at yourself. Who'd want a physical relationship with you?' He sat down on the piano seat and dismissed her with a cursory wave. 'Go away, Felicity. I want to prepare for next week's concert.'

After she'd gone, he poured himself a large whisky and sat sipping it and smiling. He'd never believed in karma — the concept that bad deeds rebound on you by some form of cosmic justice — but maybe there was something in it after all.

* * *

When Felicity Thomas emailed through the list of the choir members, Aled printed it out and pinned it to the incident board beneath the photograph.

Jack peered at it. What a disparate bunch! They were all ages from a couple of youngsters to some elderly folk with sticks and everything in between. He instructed the team. 'I want full background checks on all these people, please. I realize that Snell's killer may not be a choir member at all, but we have to start somewhere and these were the people with whom he was in regular contact and the last to see him alive apart from the killer. Flag up anything you find that's of interest, and we'll start digging.' He turned to DC Fox. 'When we interviewed Doreen Snell, who was it she suspected Charlie had sneaked off to see after choir practice?'

Gemma consulted her notes. 'Mrs Snell said, "*If I'm not there to drag him home, he's off after anything in skirts, mostly that flashy piece from the knicker shop down the road.*" I'm guessing that when she said "down the road", she meant it was on the same street as Charlie's Chop Shop, but we don't have a name.'

'The shop's called Wild Styles, Sarge.' Clive was tapping at his keyboard. 'It's owned by a Ms Roxanne Wild. According to her website, she specializes in very sexy, ultra-alluring peephole bras and sultry knickers designed to show off your silhouette.' He paused. 'Blimey, Sarge! You should see the pics!'

'Stop that at once, Clive. It'll ruin your eyesight and you're upsetting DC Fox.' Bugsy hurried over to take a look. 'I don't expect it's any worse than the things I saw when I was in the vice squad and — flippin' heck!' He beckoned to

Jack. 'I think we should pay this lady a visit, guv. After all, if Snell did go there after choir practice, she might have been the last person to see him alive.'

Jack nodded. 'I agree, Sergeant. But if we are to get a totally dispassionate and impartial report, I suggest we send DC Fox and DC Dinkley. They're less likely to be distracted by their surroundings. In the meantime, Clive, I need you to trawl through Snell's financial records. How did he afford the luxury items like his expensive car, phone and jewellery? Find out where the money came from. I doubt it was the profit from that butcher's shop.'

'I'm on it, sir.' Clive started delving, which is what he did best.

* * *

DC Gemma Fox reversed the car into a space halfway down Richington High Street. From there, she and DC 'Velma' Dinkley walked to the lower, less salubrious end of town. DC Dinkley was a serious officer, known as 'Velma' to her colleagues after the character in *Scooby-Doo*, and the penchant in the police service for assigning everyone nicknames. The similarity to the cartoon 'Velma Dinkley' was mainly due to her baggy sweaters, square horn-rimmed spectacles and her undoubted intelligence.

They walked past Charlie's Chop Shop, now with the shutters down, and with a notice in the window that read 'Closed due to bereavement'. Wild Styles was a few doors further on. The lingerie displayed on the scantily clad models in the window was just about the right side of racy for passers-by but didn't quite prepare the officers for the items on display inside. Gemma and Velma exchanged glances. Their opinions on underwear were different but, in the end, amounted to the same. As far as Velma, the forensic psychologist, was concerned, underwear was simply a collection of practical, functional garments that you wore under your clothes and they were either black or white. She couldn't see the need for purple lace bras with peepholes in them or a triangle of red silk with two strings masquerading as knickers. Quite apart from the outrageous cost of such skimpy apparel, they looked to her like they'd be most uncomfortable to wear.

Gemma, a feminist to her very core, despised the whole concept of what she considered misogynistic frippery, designed for the sole purpose of stimulating masculine appetites, and as such, she strongly disapproved. Pandering to men's baser instincts was demeaning and she believed it set women back decades to the days when they put on a clean frock and ribbons in their hair to welcome the breadwinner home for his dinner.

If Ms Wild hoped to sell anything to these two, she was about to be disappointed. Had she known it, her sales pitch couldn't have been more inappropriate. 'Hi, ladies. What are we looking for today? I've got a new line in open crotch panties. They offer easy access to your lady-garden that your partners will love.' A sudden thought struck her. These days, you had to be careful not to assign a gender to anybody, regardless of appearances. It seemed to her that you could identify as a mushroom if you were so inclined and nobody dared question it. But old habits were hard to shift. She attempted to recover the situation. 'But perhaps you two are partners?' Nobody could accuse her of ignoring diversity, or even worse, losing a potential sale because of it.

As if in response to a silent command, both officers simultaneously whipped out their warrant cards and held them up, where she could read them. 'Ms Roxanne Wild? I'm Detective Constable Fox and this is my colleague, Detective Constable Dinkley. We'd like to ask you some questions about the late Charlie Snell.'

For a split second, her face registered something akin to alarm, but she rallied gamely and the lusty shopkeeper's smile returned. 'Oh. Er . . . yes. I see. I heard on the grapevine that Charlie had been found dead in Richington Forest after choir practice. They're saying he was murdered. Is that right?'

Gemma ignored the question and asked one of her own. 'Which grapevine would that be, Ms Wild?'

'Please call me Roxy. Everyone does. It was the choir's bush telegraph. I sing mezzo-soprano,' she added, in case they were wondering about the connection. 'The choir's a kind of music mafia. Members come from all walks of life and from all over town, so there's never a lack of gossip. Nothing's sacred. But why are you questioning me? Shouldn't you be out there, catching whoever did it?'

'We're following several lines of enquiry, Madam,' said Velma. 'For example, we're trying to establish where Mr Snell went after choir practice had finished. Did he come to see you?'

'No. Why would he?' Roxy processed this for a few moments then blurted out — 'Oh, I get it! You've been talking to his wife! Doreen has some barmy idea that Charlie and I were at it, behind her back.' She gave a snort of laughter. 'In his dreams! He was an ageing, unattractive, mean-minded skinny old lech. I assure you, I can do better than that! In answer to your question, no, I didn't see him again after choir practice. I came home, had a large glass of Sauvignon Blanc in the hot tub and went to bed — on my own. Now, if that's all, officers, I have a business to run.'

Walking back to the car, Gemma asked Velma, 'You're the psychologist. Was she telling the truth do you think?'

Velma thought about it. 'On balance, yes, I think she was. But probably not the whole truth. Her facial expressions and body language implied that she knew rather more about Snell than she was prepared to divulge. But I think we can be fairly sure that she wasn't the last person to see him alive that night and I doubt very much if she plodded through the muddy forest in the pelting rain in order to clout him over the head.'

CHAPTER THREE

When Jack got home that evening, he was pleased to see his wife Corrie's green delivery van parked in the drive. He shoehorned his car alongside and let himself in the front door. Appetizing smells were coming from the kitchen, reminding him that the advantage of having a wife who owned a successful catering business was that he knew he could always be sure of a tasty supper. The disadvantages were that Coriander's Cuisine catered a lot of posh dinner parties in the evenings, which meant Corrie wasn't always home to dish up, so he had to get it out of the oven himself. It also meant that on busy nights, she drove home in one of the delivery vans instead of leaving it in the garage at the industrial unit and using her car, presenting him with a tricky parking situation. But at least she was home.

'Hello, darling. Busy day?' He kissed her on the cheek.

'Manic. How about you?' She flicked a damp curl out of her eyes.

'Same. What's for supper?' He sniffed the air like a Customs & Excise spaniel round a camper van.

'Venison casserole. I thought I'd try out that new game butcher in the high street.'

'Do you ever buy meat from Charlie's Chop Shop?'

She shook her head. 'Definitely not. I don't want to poison my customers. That place has a terrible reputation. I'm surprised the FSA hasn't closed him down. Why do you ask?'

'Well, somebody *has* closed him down — permanently. His body was found in Richington Forest this morning. He'd been bashed over the head.'

'Crikey! That's a bit extreme. I'm guessing it wasn't just somebody who bought a tough piece of steak.' She lifted a steaming cast iron casserole dish from the oven and ladled venison onto plates.

Jack's mouth was watering. He helped himself to vegetables. 'No, I suspect the motive was more complicated than that. What do you know about the Richington Community Choir?'

'Not much. Our paths have crossed at certain events when they've provided the singing, and my team has provided the refreshments. They're pretty good, actually. Why do you ask?'

'Charlie Snell was a member — basso-profundo. Apparently, his voice was the only good thing about him. He was universally disliked, even by his wife and son. It's proving difficult to find someone who *didn't* want to give him a smack. My copper's nose tells me that the choir is heavily involved somehow. It was Dr Elizabeth Amory, another member of the choir, who found the body.'

'Oh, I know her,' said Corrie confidently. 'She's on the committee of almost every organization in Kings Richington. I believe she chairs most of them. She's one of those women who can't seem to relax unless she's controlling something. They call her Busy Lizzie behind her back. And she shares her opinions on everything — very holier-than-thou and absolutely paranoid about protecting her reputation. She's a very severe magistrate too; one of the "bring back hanging" and "flogging's too good for 'em" brigade. The rumour is that she's planning to stand for mayor at the next election. She's already been out on the hustings, talking to people and drumming up support. It'll be Member of Parliament next.

I don't know how women like that find the time.' Corrie pointed to her empty glass. 'Were you going to top me up any time soon? That wine won't drink itself, you know.'

'Sorry, sweetheart.' He unscrewed the cap and glugged some Pinot Noir into their glasses.

She took a mouthful and savoured it. 'As a sommelier, you're a very good police officer, darling.'

'What does Busy Lizzie's husband do?' wondered Jack.

'Julian? I think he's a company director. I don't know which company though, but it must be doing well. They live in a smart house on the edge of town. Six beds and three receptions if I'm any judge, and any number of baths. You say she found Charlie's body?'

'Yep. It didn't seem to upset her at all, despite his head being covered in blood.'

'I don't expect it did. I'm surprised she wasn't mucking in and trying to supervise the SOCOs.'

While they ate, Corrie thought about what Jack had said regarding his copper's nose and the choir. She knew from past experience that his nose — despite being wonky and off-centre due to his rugby-playing days — was very rarely wrong. His hunches had led to the successful resolution of many difficult cases. 'If you suspect Charlie Snell's murder is somehow connected to the choir, maybe you need a spy on the inside to check it out. You know — a snitch, a stoolie, a grass . . .'

Jack grinned. 'You have a very lurid turn of phrase for an exclusive caterer to the nobs and upper classes.'

'I learned most of it from Carlene.'

As if the mention of her name had conjured her up, like a genie from a lamp, Carlene poked her head around the back door. 'I smell venison. Is there any left?'

Corrie got a plate and spooned some on to it. 'Hello, love. Late night at the bistro?'

Carlene had grown up in a local authority children's home and, at sixteen, had moved into her own flat from the halfway house for young adults, courtesy of Jack and Corrie.

Corrie was the closest she'd ever had to a real mother and had taught her how to cook and paid for her to go to catering college. Now, Carlene ran her own very successful Michelin-starred bistro Chez Carlene with her partner, Antoine, and she marched to the beat of her own drum. But she'd never forgotten how much she owed to Jack and Corrie — especially Corrie, and she loved her to bits. She wolfed down the casserole. 'This is ace, Mrs D.' Carlene had called Jack and Corrie 'Mr Jack and Mrs D' when they first took her in. It was a mark of the respect she held for them both, and despite the passing years, she had never got out of the habit. 'I haven't eaten all day. The bistro has been rammed. I had to help Antoine in the kitchen. Don't people cook their own meals anymore?'

'Don't knock it,' cautioned Corrie. 'If they did, you and I would be out of a job.' She rolled her eyes. 'And I have pledged to keep my husband in the luxurious manner to which I've foolishly allowed him to become accustomed.'

'Carlene, can you sing?' asked Jack, still considering what Corrie had said about planting a 'stoolie' in the choir.

'Well, I can do a bit of Taylor Swift on karaoke nights and my Lady Gaga isn't bad, but . . .'

'No, I mean proper singing.'

'I thought that was proper singing.' Carlene was confused.

'Jack means in a choir,' explained Corrie.

'Only at school and then I had to mime. If I sang out loud, it put the other kids off. Why do you ask?'

'It doesn't matter, Carlene, love.' Jack handed her the serving spoon. 'Have some more casserole.'

* * *

Next day at the station, Jack studied the photo of the Richington Choir members and the numbered list of names beside it. 'You know, Bugsy, we could really do with matching the names to faces to help with the background checks.

Obviously, we know Snell' — Jack wrote the number on the dead man's face on the photo — 'and we know Dr Amory.' He did the same with her.

'And that's Roxy Wild, sir.' Gemma wrote her number on her face, too.

'That's three of them identified. Only another seventeen or so to go. For that, and all sorts of other reasons, we need to get somebody into the choir, undercover. What I don't want to do is go marching in amongst them, waving warrants and asking lots of questions. That way, we'll only find out what they want us to know. Any ideas?'

Bugsy shouted across to DC Williams. 'Aled, son, can you sing?'

He stood up. 'Can I sing, Sarge?' His voice rose a few decibels in volume. 'CAN I SING? I'm a Welshman — of course I can sing.' And to prove it, he belted out, in a powerful tenor voice — *'Men of Harlech march to glory, Victory is hov'ring o'er ye, Bright-eyed freedom stands before ye, Hear ye not her call?'*

When he'd finished, the whole of the incident room gave him a rousing cheer and a round of applause.

'I sang in a male voice choir back in Pontypool, before I gave up all the fame, fortune and fornication to come here and be a detective constable. I'm guessing you want me to audition for the Richington Community lot, sir?'

'That's exactly what I want you to do, Aled,' confirmed Jack. 'Keep your eyes and ears open, put the rest of the names to these faces and report anything suspicious that you see or overhear. It's a long shot, but I'm sure Snell's killer is mixed up with that choir. I don't believe some opportunist mugged him in Richington Forest late at night and in the pouring rain. He still had all his valuables, and he didn't sustain any other injuries, just that one blow from behind with a tree branch. That wasn't a random killing — he was targeted.'

'You might want to look at this, sir?' Clive beckoned to Jack to look at the information he had pulled up from Charlie Snell's bank. 'Snell paid in large amounts of cash at regular intervals. It's not the account that was used for the butcher's shop; it's a separate one lodged with a different bank. I spoke to the manager and he said Snell would arrive with it in a brown envelope and hand it to the cashier. He claimed the money was takings from the shop, but it obviously wasn't.'

'That's a very healthy nest egg he had stashed away. Now, I wonder where he got all that cash from,' said Bugsy. 'I doubt if it was legitimate. What d'you reckon? Drugs? Gambling? Money laundering? Some other lucrative side hustle?'

'Whatever it was, I bet his wife didn't know about it,' said Jack. 'It explains how he could afford fast cars and all the other luxuries he treated himself to. I think we should pay Doreen Snell another visit, don't you, Sergeant?'

'Absolutely, guv. We need to find out more about this bloke's secret lifestyle.'

* * *

They found Doreen Snell upstairs in the flat over the butcher's shop, which was still closed due to bereavement. Bradley, her son, had come home from university and they were deciding on an appropriate coffin for Charlie once the police had released his body.

'We're sorry to bother you again at a time like this, Mrs Snell, but a few facts have come to light since we last spoke.' Jack was treading carefully. The poor woman had been through enough while Snell was alive; she was entitled to some peace now that he was dead.

She looked anxious. 'I've been and identified his body like you asked, Inspector. What more can I tell you?'

Bradley put a protective arm around his mother. 'When can we arrange my father's funeral, Inspector Dawes? Mum won't rest until it's all over and she can get her life back on track.'

It was clear to both police officers that there was no love lost between Bradley and his father, but had he hated him enough to kill him? The team had checked out his alibi. He had been at a university gig the night Charlie was murdered. Several people said they had seen him, but it had been very crowded and 'much drink had been consumed' according to his friends. These days, it wasn't impossible to get from Leicester to Kings Richington with time to commit a murder and be back in your flat while your mates were still sleeping off a hangover. But realistically, Bradley wasn't top of the list of suspects — a list that was destined to reach substantial proportions before any conclusion was reached.

'Mrs Snell, can you tell us what you know about this, please?' Bugsy showed her a printout of Snell's clandestine bank statement.

Doreen put on her reading glasses and peered at it for some time with Bradley looking over her shoulder. 'I don't understand. Are you saying Charlie had all this money in an account of his own while the business was overdrawn and I could barely pay my meat suppliers?'

'It's looking that way, Mrs Snell,' confirmed Bugsy. 'I take it you knew nothing about it?'

'No. Nothing. Where did it all come from?' It was obvious that she was genuinely astonished.

'We were hoping you could tell us,' said Jack.

Bradley was seething, pacing up and down and punching the palms of his hands. 'The miserable, mean, deceitful old bastard! He had all that cash while my mother was struggling to scratch a living in that crummy butcher's shop.' He stopped to think. 'Will Mum get the money now that the wicked old sod's dead, Inspector? She's surely entitled to something, if only to cover the cost of his funeral.'

'That would be a question for the courts, sir, but it rather depends how your father obtained the money in the first place and we still need to find that out.' Privately, Jack doubted it would have been legal, given what they knew of Charlie Snell. He stood up. 'I'm sorry to have troubled you, Mrs Snell, but you understand we need to check out everything if we're to find whoever it was that killed your husband.'

'And when you do find him,' growled Bradley, 'let me know. I want to shake his hand.'

* * *

Aled's acceptance into the Community Choir was a foregone conclusion. The audition took place in Bryn's 'music room' and was brief. Once Thomas recognized the Welsh accent and heard his vocal range, he welcomed him with open arms.

'It's good to have you, Mr Williams. Welcome to our happy band of songsters.'

'Thanks for accepting me.' Aled trod carefully. 'I heard somewhere that the choir lost one of its members recently.'

Bryn frowned. 'That's right. Snell was my basso-profundo. A great loss to the overall substance and depth of the choir but no loss to humanity.'

'Really?' probed Aled. 'Why do you say that?'

Bryn hesitated. 'Let's just say he had some unpleasant habits and leave it at that, shall we? Now, how are you fixed for a practice in the church hall tomorrow evening? We start at seven, sharp. Does that fit in with your work schedule? I don't believe you mentioned what you do for a living.'

'Oh, I'm a civil servant. Nothing special.' It wasn't really a lie, thought Aled, just bending the truth a bit, and it was important the choir didn't know they had a police detective amongst them until he'd had time to do some detecting. 'What about you, Bryn? What do you do when you're not conducting choir business?'

'I have a very important managerial job in retail distribution. You see, Mr Williams, a good distribution strategy involves understanding your product's target market segments, their location and the transportation logistics around creation and delivery. I also have to calculate the capacity of the profit margin to divide profit between multiple intermediate steps.' He gave what he thought was a modest shrug. 'It would be no exaggeration to say that the company would go under without my expertise.'

'Yes, I'm sure.' Aled was unimpressed. In his view, the man was an opinionated arse.

'Right, Mr Williams. We'll see you tomorrow evening.' Bryn showed him out.

Concealed behind the kitchen door, Felicity jumped out at Bryn when he came past. 'Why did you tell him that? You don't have an important managerial job; you're a dogsbody, a lackey. And you wouldn't have a job at all if you hadn't lied on the job application.'

'Felicity, I do wish you wouldn't keep eavesdropping on my private conversations. What I say and do is none of your business. It's very annoying!' He was red in the face with temper. 'One of these days, I shall . . .'

'You'll do what, Bryn? Hit me? Throw me out? I think we both know that you daren't do either of those things.' She shut the kitchen door firmly in his face.

* * *

Back at the station, Aled reported to DI Dawes. 'Right, sir, I'm in. There's a practice tomorrow at seven and I shall be introduced to the choir as a newcomer.'

'Well done, Aled. See what you can find out.'

'You know, guv,' said Bugsy, 'I'm still having doubts about Dr Amory.'

'Is it still your favourite theory that the person who found the body is usually the murderer? I think you're barking up the wrong tree.'

'Think about it, guv. Humour me. She's an intelligent, educated woman. She'll know that we all shed DNA all the time, leaving traces of our identity practically everywhere we go. Big Ron says however careful a murderer is not to leave any traces behind, there's always some minute fragment of forensic material that can be identified to catch him out. So if, after you've done the deed, you come back to the scene and pretend to "find" the body, it would explain why there are traces of your DNA, fingerprints and so on.'

'You have a point, Bugsy, but what would be her motive? I very much doubt whether Snell was daft enough to try anything unpleasant with her. She clearly regarded him as some kind of flesh-eating Neanderthal.'

'Yeah, I expect you're right, guv. It was just a thought.'

CHAPTER FOUR

Aled arrived at the church hall early, keen to get started on his undercover work to put names to faces. The choir members were a small but friendly bunch and introduced themselves to the new guy as they arrived. Fortunately, Aled had a good memory and was able to remember most of their identities.

'Hi, you must be Mr Williams.' A man Aled estimated to be in his forties shook his hand. He was casually dressed in black jeans and a white polo neck shirt and had the sort of slick hair style you see in posh barbers' windows. 'Fliss sent us all an email to expect a new member tonight. I'm Geoff Smart. I own Smart's Autos on the bypass. If you're ever in need of a good, reliable used car, I'm your man. Funding options to suit every pocket.'

'Thanks,' replied Aled. 'I'll remember.'

'Ah, here's Roxy. She's a good sport. Lovely full-bodied . . . er . . . mezzo-soprano. We . . . er . . . hook up, occasionally.' He winked. 'I'll introduce you.'

Aled had heard Gemma and Velma's account of Roxy Wild, with instructions to keep his distance if he didn't want to be eaten alive. He could see what they meant. He guessed Roxy was what his grannie Gwynedd in Pontypool would describe as 'no better than she ought to be'. She wore a low-cut scarlet top with skin-tight black leather trousers and far too much make-up. Her dark hair fell in long glamorous curls, framing her face and belying her age. Given Gemma's description of the items on sale in her shop, he could only speculate about what she might be wearing underneath. Hastily, he put it out of his mind.

Roxy spotted him and homed in like a heat-seeking drone. 'Hey there. I'm Roxy and you're our new recruit. I'm very pleased to meet you, sweetie.'

Aled swallowed hard. 'Hello.' To his embarrassment, the word came out in falsetto.

She laughed — a rich, throaty gurgle. 'Don't tell me we have a Barry Gibb on the strength! That should expand the choir's repertoire a bit.'

Aled coughed. 'No, sorry. Bit of a dry throat. I'm a tenor, actually.'

'What you need is a drink,' declared Geoff. 'A few of us meet in the Richington Arms after practice for a quick one. Jim, the landlord, is in the choir, excellent baritone. You could join us if you like.'

That, thought Aled, could pose a threat to his cover. Jim would have seen him in the pub with other police officers on a Friday night, relaxing after a particularly hectic week. He would need to get to him first and warn him not to say anything. He realized it was going to be tricky working undercover on his own patch. While he was thinking about the best way to do it without drawing attention to himself, Bryn Thomas swept in with Felicity close behind, weighed down with all the paraphernalia necessary for the practice. She stumbled and dropped some sheets of music.

'Oh do come along, Felicity,' Bryn scolded. 'We haven't got all night while you blunder about throwing the music around.'

Several choir members helped her pick it up, including Geoff. He whispered to Aled, 'I feel sorry for poor Fliss — what she puts up with from that arsehole. I don't know why she doesn't leave him. They've no children. She doesn't owe him anything.'

There wasn't time for more chat as Bryn called the choir to order, and they shuffled into their usual formation. 'I'd like to introduce our new tenor, Aled Williams,' Bryn declared with a flourish. 'I'm sure you will all make him feel at home. He comes from a background of Welsh male voice choirs, so he will prove a valuable member of our little ensemble.' He spoke directly to Aled. 'I'd like you on the end of this row, please.' He pointed to a space and Aled shuffled into it. 'As one of our stronger singers, I need you to provide support and stability to our overall sound. It allows for a more cohesive blend and balance within the choir.'

After the first few songs, Aled began to enjoy himself. Despite Bryn's pompous approach, he guessed they weren't into any highbrow stuff, just popular pieces they could perform at community functions, which was fine. He could read the music, no problem. One particular song — 'Somewhere Over the Rainbow' — included a solo sung by a young lady with a beautiful, clear coloratura soprano voice. Her high notes were superb and her timbre impressive, brighter and more sparkling than any of the other sopranos. Aled couldn't see who she was without turning around, so he waited for the tea break to ask Geoff.

'Who was that singing the solo?'

'That's young Ellie — Eloise Bishop — over there, by the tea trolley.' He pointed to a young, fresh-faced teenager wearing skinny jeans and a sweater. 'She's our star performer. Only seventeen and destined for much greater things than singing with this gang of tone-deaf losers. Her parents encouraged her to have singing lessons to help with her asthma, never realizing how good she'd turn out.'

'That young man with her . . .' Aled cast his mind back to when the choir members introduced themselves at the start of the evening. '. . . that's Luke Burton, if I remember rightly.'

'Yep. Poor lad's nuts about her, but I doubt she'll stay here in Kings Richington after she finishes college. It's a pity, really, because Luke is a solitary lad — brought up in care and a series of foster homes. He has a steady job in the garden centre, but what he really needs is a loving relationship.' He laughed. 'Don't we all? Luke used to keep Charlie Snell away from her. The dirty old sod was always stalking her during practices. I know it's bad luck to speak ill of the dead, but I'm sure in Snell's case, bad luck will make an exception.'

'Young man . . .'

Aled felt a tap on his arm. He turned to see an elderly white-haired lady, the top of her head just above his elbow. She was dressed almost entirely in different shades of purple — plum trousers, frilly lilac blouse and a hand-knitted mauve wrap — and she smelled strongly of lavender.

'. . . my name is Dibble . . . Violet Dibble. I hope you'll stay with us and not leave when you get fed up, like all the others. We need more young voices like yours.'

Violet Dibble had to be at least eighty, Aled decided, and he guessed she was responsible for the high-pitched, tremulous vibrato he'd heard, coming from somewhere in the centre of the ensemble. The quavering soprano descant appeared to be singing something different to everyone else and Aled couldn't begin to guess what key she was in. Nevertheless, she was what community was all about and he took her hand. 'I'm very pleased to meet you, Mrs Dibble. Is your husband in the choir, too?'

'No. Robert died some years ago.' She whispered conspiratorially, 'He was a lousy singer, anyway, bless him. Couldn't carry a tune in a bucket. I doubt if he's making much of an impression on the heavenly choir. Shall we get a cup of tea?' They made their way to the trolley. 'I believe there are rock buns tonight. Felicity's rock buns are notorious, you might say eponymous, more rock than bun — watch your teeth. She does her best, but being married to that Welsh cretin can't be conducive to culinary excellence. No offence to the Welsh; I'm sure you're not all cretins. You only have to look at Llywelyn ap Gruffudd, Lloyd George and Tom Jones.'

Aled grinned. As a police officer, his experience of elderly ladies was that they were a fertile source of information and local gossip, both recent and past, and especially of the gruesome kind. He decided to find out. 'You must have been shocked to hear of Charlie Snell's murder.'

Her face froze. 'Why? What have you heard? What have people been saying?'

Aled was surprised at her reaction. 'Nothing, Mrs Dibble, only that his body had been found in Richington Forest by a member of the choir. I believe the details were reported in the *Echo*.'

'Well, it had nothing to do with me, young man.' She took her tea and her rock bun and walked unsteadily away.

Aled wondered what that was all about. If she'd been young and strong, he might have considered her reaction to be a sign of guilt or, at the very least, involvement. But he doubted she'd be able to even lift an oak branch, let alone wallop someone over the head with it. And he didn't fancy her chances in the forest at night in a rainstorm. So why the defensive attitude? Very odd!

While he was still mulling it over, Dr Amory burst in through the swing doors and hurried up to the tea trolley. 'Oh, good, I'm not too late for tea.' She sloshed some into a mug and grabbed a bun. 'Sorry I'm late, everybody — had to chair a meeting of the Bricklayers Guild. They go on a bit. What have I missed?'

Bryn Thomas took her to one side and brought her up to date with what had been practised so far and how her contralto input had been sorely missed.

'What the hell does Busy Lizzie know about bricklaying?' Roxy had sidled up and stood close enough to Aled for him to become enveloped in her perfume, which was definitely not lavender. It was heady, lingering and slightly hypnotic, like the wearer. 'Beats me how she gets accepted into all these organizations. She only does it for the publicity. She's running for mayor next year, would you believe?'

'Yes,' said Aled, edging away slightly so that there was more than a fag paper's distance between them. 'I had heard something of the sort.' He'd seen it in the background check on Dr Amory that Clive had produced.

'She never comes into my shop. I bet she wears those big flannel drawers with a pocket in the leg for her hankie. Are you coming to the pub afterwards? You can buy me a drink.'

Aled was torn. Part of him was reluctant to go in case it blew his cover. On the other hand, pubs were excellent places for finding things out by observation and listening in to other peoples' conversations. 'Er . . . yes, OK.'

After choir practice, when everyone was putting on their coats, Aled approached Jim Scuttle. 'Jim, can I have a word?'

'Hi, Aled, mate. Good to see you in the choir. I could hear your rich Welsh vocals above all the other noise in that section. Has DI Dawes let you have the evening off?'

'Er . . . actually, Jim, I'd rather you didn't mention that I'm a cop on the Murder Investigation Team.'

'Oh, I get it. You're working undercover on the Charlie Snell case. Well, good luck with that. I can name a dozen folk that are glad he's gone. Me for one.'

Aled was curious. 'Why, Jim?' Jim Scuttle was the classic 'mine host', full of bonhomie and good nature. He had taken over the Richington Arms from the previous landlord relatively recently and had been well-accepted. Even when he was chucking people out, he did it with a smile and a friendly warning.

Jim lowered his voice. 'Trust me, Aled. He was a nasty piece of work. I don't know exactly what he was up to — if I had, I'd have reported him to your people — but I've seen him sitting in the corner with some very shady characters and a lot of cash was changing hands. On one occasion, a fight nearly broke out.'

'If you'd told us you suspected him of something illegal, we'd have kept an eye on him.'

'Yeah, I wish I had now. Anyway, watch your back, mate. Now he's been murdered, there could be repercussions.'

The drink in the pub was brief, with most choir members either going straight home or having a swift half before getting a takeaway to eat watching the football on telly or a recording of their favourite soap. Bryn and Felicity Thomas didn't join them, neither did Mrs Dibble, Dr Amory or Luke — Ellie being too young to accompany him.

When Aled went to the bar to order drinks, Jim leant towards him as he handed them over and whispered, 'Don't look now, but I recognize those two blokes in the alcove wearing black hoodies. They're the ones who met Snell here on a couple of occasions. The big bald one with the tattoos was the one who started shouting and looked like he was going to punch him.'

'You don't know their names or where they come from, I suppose?' asked Aled hopefully.

''Fraid not, mate, but I'm pretty sure they're not locals. They don't talk to anyone but each other and in a foreign language that I don't recognize. Could be Turkish, could be Albanian.'

'Might they be on your CCTV?'

'No, it doesn't cover that secluded part of the pub. I expect that's why they sit there. You might catch a glimpse on the camera outside when they leave. Sorry.' Jim moved away to the other end of the bar and carried on serving drinks.

Ideally, Aled would have liked to speak to the men, ask them their names, but if, as Jim suspected, they were up to something illegal, identifying himself as a copper wouldn't help him to find out what it was. In fact, it would put them on their guard and they were bound to lie then leg it. Instead, under the guise of making a call, he took out his phone and photographed them. It wasn't a very good shot, but with any luck, Clive might be able to trace them on his unofficial rogues' gallery.

As they were leaving, Roxy kissed him goodnight on the cheek and whispered in his ear, 'If you ever want a glamorous gift for a girlfriend, come to my shop on the high street. I'm sure I could find something sexy and exciting that would interest you.'

Well, thought Aled as he walked home. *She's got some nerve!* She had to be as old as his auntie Delyth. But was she a possible suspect for Snell's murder? He knew from her grip on his arm that she'd be strong enough and she'd made it clear that Charlie was one man whose advances she definitely did not encourage. What was it she'd called him? — an ageing, unattractive, mean-minded skinny old lech. Velma had said she felt Roxy knew rather more about Snell than she'd been prepared to divulge when she was interviewed, and Velma's intuitions were rarely wrong. But was whatever she knew a strong enough motive to follow him into the forest after choir practice and kill him? He thought not.

* * *

Next morning, Aled wrote the numbers on the list of the choir members' names against their faces on the whiteboard. He also emailed the photograph he'd taken of the ruffians in the pub to Clive, who wasn't too optimistic about establishing their identities but promised he'd give it his best shot. Some choir members, for reasons of age or infirmity, were clearly not realistic candidates to follow anyone into the forest at night in a storm and commit a violent act, so although Clive did cursory background checks, they were never going to be serious contenders.

'Right, folks . . .' Jack called the team to the whiteboard. '. . . let's look at who we have in the theoretical frame at the moment. We'll start at the top — Bryn Thomas, choirmaster. It's no secret that Thomas didn't like Snell, but then, nobody did, so that alone isn't really a motive.'

'Bryn and his wife, Felicity, both have alibis.' DC Chippendale was keen to be seen to contribute, rather than just sit and listen. 'According to their statements . . .' He checked the notes on his computer. '. . . they went straight home after choir practice and were in bed just after ten.'

'OK, Chippy, and so far, we've no reason to doubt that they're telling the truth?' Bugsy asked.

'No, Sarge. Thomas has a managerial position in distribution, and Mrs Thomas used to be a primary school teacher. She gave it up after her parents died and left her their house.'

'I haven't been able to verify any of that yet, sir,' declared Clive.

'Fair enough, but they don't strike me as a modern-day Bonnie and Clyde, so we'll take them at face value for now.' Jack pointed to Geoff Smart. 'What did you make of this chap, Aled?'

'Very friendly. Owns a used-car business on the bypass. Bit of a ladies' man. Having an occasional thing with Ms Roxanne Wild and feels sorry for Mrs Thomas. Thinks the way Bryn Thomas treats her justifies her kicking him out. He has an alibi for Snell's murder. He was in the pub with the rest of them, then after a swift half, he went back to his garage to do some paperwork.'

'Smart's business is sound, as far as I can see, sir,' added Clive. 'Good turnover, nothing dodgy with his accounts. CCTV outside his garage confirms him arriving around ten thirty and leaving after midnight, so he wouldn't have had time to go to Richington Forest and kill Snell.'

'Again, he didn't rate Charlie Snell, but that in itself doesn't constitute a motive. If it did, most of Kings Richington would be under suspicion,' said Jack. 'How did you get on with Roxanne Wild, Aled? We still don't have proof that Snell didn't visit her after choir practice as his wife suspected.'

'I think it's unlikely, sir, and she certainly wouldn't have gone to meet him in the forest. She may be a little free with her favours . . .' He heard Gemma muttering 'judgemental' behind him. '. . . but she has standards and Snell would not have met them. More to the point, there was no sign of him on the CCTV outside her shop.'

'Of course,' said Jack, 'we shouldn't ignore the possibility that he could have been killed by someone who isn't anything to do with the choir. His wife, his son, the shady characters he used to meet in the pub — get digging, team.'

CHAPTER FIVE

Downstairs on the desk, Sergeant Parsloe was deep in thought. There had been a spate of fake passports circulating in Kings Richington and top brass were keen to find out who was responsible and put them out of business. The National Crime Agency press release had been firm and unambiguous:

> *Those looking to profit from illicit activities have no place in our community and we remain committed to dismantling these organized criminal operations and ensuring those believed to be involved get an early call from the law enforcement authorities.*

The NCA had stressed that fake passports carried a national threat of high-level criminals evading arrest and identification, never mind enabling illegals and drug smugglers to travel here who shouldn't be in this country at all. According to the brief Norman had received, individuals were being paid for expired passports, and these were then renewed using photographs of criminals who were willing to pay up to ten thousand pounds to start new lives. He was trawling his mental database trying to think which of Kings Richington's criminal blacklist might be involved, but so far, he'd drawn a blank. It was clearly a lucrative business and beyond the wit of the petty crooks who kept cropping up on his watch. Amid this wool-gathering, he became aware of an elderly lady on the other side of the desk, needing his attention. 'Yes, Madam. How can I help you?'

'My name is Mrs Dibble — Violet Dibble — that's spelled D-I-B-B-L-E. Are you writing this down, officer? I've come to make a statement.'

'I see, Mrs Dibble. And what would you like to make a statement about?'

'It's about the murder of Charlie Snell. The police will find out eventually, so I decided that the best thing was to give myself up.'

Norman was torn between astonishment and amusement, but he kept a straight face. 'Are you saying that you did it, Mrs Dibble?'

She became indignant. 'No, of course not! Do I look as if I could whack someone over the head with a lump of wood? But along with a lot of other people, I had a very good motive, so I guessed you people would arrest me on suspicion when you found out about it. And I don't fancy spending time in your chokey while you eliminate me from your enquiries.' She pushed a back copy of the *Richington Echo* across the desk with a small paragraph circled in red. 'Here — that will explain it.'

Sergeant Parsloe was acutely aware of his responsibilities as a public servant, especially where little old ladies were concerned. Nowadays, it wasn't enough just to help them across the road; they expected and deserved an intelligent response from the police when they had a problem. He read the paragraph she had highlighted. Then he read it again. 'I'm sorry, Mrs Dibble, but I don't quite understand. This article says Charlie Snell ran over your coat in his butcher's van. Was your coat lying in the road or were you wearing it at the time?'

'What?' Mrs Dibble snatched the paper back, put on the spectacles hanging around her neck on a chain and peered at it. 'Oh, for goodness' sake! Doesn't anybody at the *Echo* ever proofread these articles?' She grabbed a pen off the desk, scribbled out one letter and pushed the newspaper back.

'Oh, I see.' Norman frowned. 'Snell ran over your *cat*. I'm very sorry.'

'Yes. Poor Pavarotti. He was getting on, like me, and couldn't run out of the way fast enough. And you people did nothing. Snell got away with it.'

'Unfortunately, Mrs Dibble, at the present time, running over a cat doesn't have to be reported and it isn't a criminal offence. We like to think people will do the decent thing, but they don't always . . .'

She sniffed disdainfully. 'There was nothing decent about Charlie Snell, Sergeant. He deserved what he got. I like to think it was Pavarotti's revenge. Anyway, I thought you should know that it wasn't I who murdered the ghastly man. Good day to you.' She turned to leave when Aled suddenly appeared on the station side of the desk, behind Norman.

'Sergeant Parsloe, do you know anything about . . . ?' He stopped. 'Oh . . . hello . . . Mrs Dibble,' he stammered. 'Fancy seeing you here.'

'That's just what I was thinking, Mr Williams.' She gave him a reproachful look. 'You're a police officer?'

Aled glanced at Norman, whose face was expressionless. 'I'm a detective constable, actually. Why don't you come through, Mrs Dibble?' Aled unlocked the door. 'I'm sure you could do with a cup of tea and we can have a chat.'

After a mug of strong tea, several biscuits and an explanation, Mrs Dibble forgave Aled for the subterfuge. 'So you're an undercover agent. How exciting.'

'Not really, Violet. I'm just trying to find out more about the choir members without putting them under pressure.'

'Well, I can help you there.' She took another biscuit. 'You'd be surprised what people reveal in front of elderly ladies. We're invisible, you see.' She had a light bulb idea. 'I could be your deputy.'

Aled wondered what can of worms he may have inadvertently opened and whether it might be possible to close it again. 'Thank you, Violet, but I wouldn't want you to go to any trouble.'

'Oh, it's no trouble, Agent Williams. I shall be your eyes and ears.' She put three fingers against her forehead in the Girl Guide's salute and beamed. 'Officer Dibble at your service.'

* * *

Detective Chief Superintendent George Garwood was away in Harrogate at a senior police officers' conference for another week. The prospectus had promised 'thought-provoking sessions and discussions exploring effective practices and identifying solutions to emerging challenges and leading change in the police service for the common good'.

Jack was keen to have the Snell murder resolved and the killer in custody before Garwood came back, because after such meetings with his peers, he always returned in a bad mood with a hangover and indigestion. At the moment things weren't looking too hopeful.

As usual, the politically trendy editor of the *Richington Echo* had pilloried the police, asking what they were doing to keep the community safe from thugs lurking in public places and implying that too much of the taxpayers' money was being spent on 'jollies for the boys'. This was a direct swipe at DCS Garwood, with whom he'd had an ongoing feud for years. Nobody could remember how it had started, but it was thought to be a dispute over a lost golf ball accompanied by angry accusations of cheating.

Jack called a team meeting to get an update on the information they had so far. The team called it a WAWA meeting — Where Are We At. Jack stood at the front, ready to write on the whiteboard.

'OK. New information, anybody?'

'Would you believe that two of our suspects have form, sir?' Clive had been delving into police records. 'Bradley Snell, the deceased's son, was arrested under the Police, Crime, Sentencing and Courts Act for joining a student protest against global warming. The report maintains that he climbed on the Weather Symbols Statues in the city — apparently, they change colour to react with the actual weather — and he urinated on the sun, turning it green. He was held in a police cell overnight, then released.' There was subdued sniggering around the room.

'I guess we can put that down to a student prank rather than inciting a full-scale environmental riot.' Jack wrote it under Bradley's name on the board. 'Who's the other one?'

'I think this one will surprise you, sir. Bryn Thomas, the choirmaster, served two years for assault, occasioning actual bodily harm, and he was ordered to undergo an anger management course.'

'Blimey! What did he do?' asked Bugsy.

'He punched a bus driver. Broke his jaw, knocked out two teeth and fractured his eye socket. Some altercation about the bus driver cutting him up at a roundabout and driving him off the road. He pursued the bus to the next stop, then dragged the driver out of the cab and clouted him in the face.'

'I thought he had a short fuse, but that's going a bit far.' Aled recalled seeing Bryn go red in the face and clench his fists if anyone as much as hinted he might be mistaken about the timing of a piece of music.

'I'm surprised he got a top job in retail with a conviction for ABH,' mused Velma.

'Maybe he didn't declare it and they didn't bother to check his credentials. It happens.' Jack noted it down on the board.

'I checked Thomas's personal bank account, sir.' Clive tapped a few keys. 'If he's a top executive in retail distribution for a leading international company, like he claims, they aren't paying him very much. He's on minimum wage. He has a joint account with his wife, though, and there's loads of dosh in that.'

'Do we know which company he works for?' asked Jack.

'Yes, sir. I've emailed it to you.'

'I think Bugsy and I might pay them a visit. If Thomas lied about his job, we need to know if there's anything else he's been lying about.'

'Sir, are we absolutely sure Doreen Snell didn't murder her husband?' DC Chippendale asked. 'She admits she went out to find him after she'd fixed the freezer in the shop but says he'd already left the church hall, so she went home. What if she didn't go home? Suppose she spotted him making for the forest and followed him to see what he was up to? Maybe she knew about the money and decided to get rid of a feckless husband and get her hands on his cash at the same time.'

'It's an interesting theory, Chippy, and it's true she was shocked when we broke the news that he was dead, but she didn't seem overcome with grief,' agreed Jack.

'Maybe she was shocked because she didn't expect the body to be found quite so quickly in a dense part of the forest,' added Bugsy. 'And she's certainly strong enough to pick up a tree branch and bash someone with it. You only need to see her with a meat cleaver.'

'Clive, see if you can get any CCTV footage of her walking home on the night of the murder,' said Jack. 'My instinct is that she didn't kill Snell, but you know what I always say — if in doubt . . .'

'Check it out!' shouted everyone in the room.

Jack smiled his approval. 'To summarize, we have a few possibles in the running, but no one stands out as a main suspect yet. It's late. Go home, enjoy your weekend and we'll have another crack at it on Monday.'

* * *

On Friday night, Felicity Thomas posted the following notice on the Richington Community Choir blog:

> *Here are a few photos from last month's joint concert with the Peasmould Fishermen's Choir, which was held inside the Peasmould Fish Market, in aid of that splendid marine*

conservation charity, Help For Haddock. We raised £45.72 from a very generous audience of at least twenty people. Our two choirs performed individually and combined together for two favourite sea shanties.

A huge thank you to everyone for making the night such a huge success. To the person who lost an upper set of dentures during the audience participation in 'Blow the Man Down', please collect them from Mrs Felicity Thomas.

On Sunday, we shall be raising funds for our local charities at Richington Garden Centre. We would love you to join us and hopefully join in the singing throughout the day whilst stocking up on your hostas and hebes.

* * *

Saturday morning saw Corrie Dawes and George Garwood's wife, Cynthia, sitting at a window table in Chez Carlene. The bistro, with its glazed brick facade in cool tones of sea-green and blue, was situated in the trendy food and drink quarter of Kings Richington. French accordion music played softly in the background while they drank good coffee and devoured diet-busting pastries. They had been friends since their schooldays and bonded at the age of twelve when Cynthia accidentally smashed Corrie's kneecap with a lacrosse stick. According to Corrie, her kneecap had 'floated' ever since. The two were not averse to a bit of unorthodox sleuthing when they felt their husbands could do with some help with a tricky case. Needless to say, it was always dangerous and mostly did more harm than good.

'Have you seen the report of Charlie Snell's murder in the *Echo*?' asked Cynthia. 'Their new crime correspondent must be about ninety. She writes everything up like an Agatha Christie mystery. She says, "*It is believed*" — she doesn't say by whom, of course — "*that master butcher, Mr Charles Snell, icon of the Richington Community Choir, was set upon by a gang of antisocial ruffians who are terrorizing our town and the police are powerless to do anything about it.*" What a load of cobblers! I don't believe that for a moment. I bet your Jack and his MIT are sprinting about like Usain Bolt, looking for the killer.'

'Well, they're certainly putting in the hours. Aled has infiltrated the choir to get the low-down on the singers.'

'Aled — is he the good-looking Welsh detective constable who nearly got sacrificed by that demon worshipper and then almost hanged himself reconstructing an alleged suicide?'

'Yep. That's the one. Health and Safety would have had a fit. It was OK though. Jack and Bugsy grabbed his legs, Velma shinned up the tree and cut him down, and Gemma drove him to hospital to have his broken fingers seen to. It was a team effort and they proved it was murder and not suicide, which was the object of the exercise. Jack says Aled's a bit accident-prone but an innovative detective constable.'

'He'll be an innovative dead one if he carries on like that. Speaking of the Community Choir, I see they're singing at the Richington Garden Centre on Sunday. Do you fancy going? I'm at a bit of a loose end with George away at his senior coppers' booze-up — I mean, diversity conference — in Harrogate. We could sing a bit and find out how to prune our perennials or whatever it is Monty Don says we're supposed to do at this time of year. What do you think?'

'Yes, OK. It'll be a nice, peaceful afternoon.'

Afterwards, Corrie was to remember those fateful words when the 'nice, peaceful afternoon' turned into a ghastly nightmare.

* * *

Judging by the crowds in the garden centre pushing trolleys piled high with plants and shrubs, Aled decided that Napoleon was wrong — England isn't a nation of shopkeepers; it's a nation of gardeners. He could see how such centres had evolved in terms of customer experience. They were now leisure destinations, places you took the family for an afternoon out rather than somewhere you went just to pick up a few bedding plants and a sack of compost. The packed cafés and play areas were proof of that, because he couldn't imagine all these people had come just to listen to the choir.

Bryn Thomas, sweating profusely, likened his attempt at shepherding his choristers to herding cats. As fast as he lined them up, someone would dash off to buy a 'particularly fine floribunda' because they were 'selling out fast'. Practice nights in the church hall were so much easier with no distractions apart from Felicity fussing with the tea trolley and the vicar 'popping in to see how they were getting on'. Bryn called the choir to order, and finally, they were assembled on the platform specially erected for them. Accompanied by much flamboyant flailing of arms from Bryn, they began by belting out a robust version of 'Whisky in the Jar', with Aled taking the lead and members of the public joining in the chorus.

'Aled's good, isn't he?' commented Corrie. She and Cynthia had found seats close to the front and were sipping cocktails from the restaurant bar.

'Handsome, too,' mused Cynthia appreciatively. 'Look at those muscles. I wonder if he'd be interested in coming and singing a few songs at my Ladies' Luncheon Club.'

Corrie glared at her. 'You wouldn't dare.'

'Oh yes I would. They'd love him.'

'They'd terrify him! You forget I've catered at some of your Ladies' Luncheon Clubs. I know what they're like, especially after a few glasses of Prosecco.'

Cynthia sighed. 'I suppose you're right. Pity though.'

* * *

All went well until after the tea break. Bryn called his choir together once more, ready for the opening number of the second half. As usual, they were to kick off with 'The Lion Sleeps Tonight', which was Luke Burton's solo. His counter-tenor voice was perfect for the song with the rest of the choir supplying the acapella Zulu chant *A-wimoweh-A-wimoweh* with claps and finger snapping as backup and Ellie providing the soprano element. It was a crowd pleaser and always went down well, whatever the venue. There were often demands for an encore.

'Luke, where are you?' shouted Bryn. 'It's your solo — you're on — now!' He looked around. 'Where has the wretched boy gone? I do wish people wouldn't keep wandering off. It's so unprofessional!'

'Maybe he got lost,' suggested someone.

Bryn bridled. 'He can't have got lost — he works here, for goodness' sake!'

'He told me he was going to meet a friend during the tea break, Maestro.' Ellie was hesitant, not wanting to get Luke into trouble. 'He said it wouldn't take long and he'd be back for his solo. I've tried to ring him, but his phone's switched off.' She didn't mention that Luke had also said he'd had some really good news — news that would change his life forever. He'd promised to explain later, when they were alone. She had no idea what it could be about, but it was clearly important to him.

'Well, he had no business fraternizing with friends during an official engagement,' snapped Bryn, 'and anyway, that was half an hour ago. Has anybody seen him since?' There was no answer, so it was apparent that nobody had. 'They must have a public address system in this place for lost children and the like. Felicity, get them to put out a message for Luke to report to the choirmaster immediately. This is most inconvenient. It will totally upset my running order.'

Felicity hurried off and Bryn faffed about, preparing the choir to sing a couple of ad hoc folk songs to fill in.

Aled felt a tap on his elbow. He looked down.

'Officer Dibble reporting for duty, Detective Williams.' She held three fingers to her forehead in her Girl Guide salute.

Aled sighed. 'Hello, Violet.'

'I think I saw young Luke going outside into the yard, where they store things like sheds and greenhouses and concrete statues. I'm going to go and look for him in case he's had some kind of accident. He could have passed out or fallen over. It isn't like him to let the choir down.' She plodded off through the crowd.

Aled called after her anxiously. 'Violet, actually I think you should stay here . . .' At the far end of the spacious outdoor part of the garden centre, he'd noticed a full-sized ornamental pond with a working fountain where they sold pumps and water lilies and the like. If she stumbled in face first and drowned, it would be his fault. He wondered if he should go after her, but Bryn was already counting him in to 'Sospan Fach'. The song was in Welsh, so nobody else could take the solo, and it had close associations with Aled's rugby club back in Pontypool, so he felt honour-bound to sing. He'd find Violet afterwards.

As it turned out, there was no need — she found him. Her small, wrinkled face was ashen and her eyes, usually bright like a bird's, were clouded with shock. She stumbled through the crowd until she reached Aled and grabbed his arm, pulling him away from the others. He supported her to stop her from tottering over. 'Detective Williams, you have to come quickly. I've found Luke.'

'What is it, Violet?' Aled was worried. 'Is he hurt?'

'Worse than that.' She struggled to speak, her breath wheezing from her lungs. 'He's dead. He's been stabbed.'

CHAPTER SIX

Aled's first instinct was to go and check it out. Violet was smart, but he had to admit she was elderly — she could be mistaken, although he couldn't see how. A dead body is a dead body, however old you are. She made to go with him, but he took her arm and guided her to a Balinese cushioned egg chair in the garden furniture section. 'No, you stay here, Violet. You've had a nasty shock. Just tell me where you found Luke and I'll go and see to it.'

'Yes, but what about . . . ?'

'I'll come back and tell you everything after I've sorted it out, I promise.'

She sank down onto the chair with relief and swayed about for a few moments while she gathered her wits. 'He's in one of the sheds. It's a light brown one made of cedar wood, about fourth or fifth on the left as you go into the yard.'

Violet might be getting on, thought Aled, but you couldn't fault her thought processes. 'What made you look inside that particular shed, Violet?'

She gulped and swallowed hard. 'I saw blood seeping out from under the door. I opened it and there he was, slumped against the slats as if he'd been dumped there. The blood had come from a wound in his chest and soaked right through his tee-shirt. I didn't touch him because it was obvious he was dead and there was nothing I could do.' She stifled a sob. 'Poor Luke, he was so young. Why would anyone do that to him?'

'I don't know, Violet, but you can be sure we'll find out. Did you close the door again?'

'Yes. I didn't want all and sundry staring at him.'

'You've been very brave. Now you stay here and rest until I come back, Officer Dibble.' He patted her hand and gave her the three-fingered salute. Aled hoped he could keep things low key until he'd had a look. He didn't want the choir and the garden centre customers panicking. As he passed Corrie and Cynthia, sipping their cocktails, he murmured to Corrie, 'Could you please keep an eye on that elderly lady over there, Mrs Dawes? She's had a nasty shock and I'm not sure she doesn't need an ambulance. If she keels over or has a heart attack or something, could you call one?'

'Yes, of course, Aled.' Corrie was alarmed. 'What's happened?'

'There's been an incident and I'm going to check it out. I don't want to alert the rest of the choir yet, but they're getting ready to leave on the coach, and if the incident is what I think it is, I might need to keep them here. Where is the inspector this afternoon?'

'He's at home, watching the rugby. Why? Do you want me to call him?'

'Not yet, thanks. It might be nothing.' But Aled had a very strong feeling that it was definitely something. He strode briskly down the store to the automatic sliding doors and out into the yard. It was empty as everybody, including the staff, was inside waiting for a final encore from the choir. Moments later, he stopped in front of the cedar shed where a trickle of blood had run through the gap under the door and congealed onto the concrete. Since he had no protective gloves, he pulled off the sash that choir members wore over their tee-shirts, wrapped it over his hand and eased open the door.

Luke Burton had been stabbed to death and his body lay limp against the shed wall, thrown in there like a discarded guy on Bonfire Night. Aled looked at him for some moments, his long forgotten Methodist upbringing coming suddenly to the surface in the face of a callous, heartless death. He murmured a few words, then he sprang into action and pulled out his phone.

* * *

DI Dawes, wearing his favourite baggy sweater and scruffy jeans, was lounging on the sofa watching the rugby. It had been a very close game, and the result hinged upon the success of the fly-half to convert a try. The player hesitated, deciding whether to attempt a place kick or a drop kick. The suspense was tangible. Two more points would clinch it. Jack had been about to open a bottle of his favourite real ale but paused, bottle in one hand and opener in the other, holding his breath for the outcome. Then his phone rang, cutting through the tension. The ringtone was the police siren that Corrie had downloaded so he'd be able to tell work calls from private ones, which meant it was work and he'd have to answer it. He put the bottle down. 'Dawes here.'

'Sir, this is DC Williams. I'm sorry to bother you on a Sunday afternoon, only we have an incident.'

'Aled. I thought you were singing with the choir at the garden centre. What happened? Did the crowd turn ugly and start chucking pot plants?' He chuckled.

'No, sir. There's a body in one of the garden sheds. He's been stabbed. It's Luke Burton, another member of the choir.'

'Right.' Jack fell instantly into work mode. He turned off the TV, noticing briefly that the fly-half had just missed the conversion. 'Stay there and secure the area. I'll be there as soon as I can.' Jack phoned Sergeant Malone, who was outside in his garage, hands covered in grease, mending his step-grandson James's bicycle. 'Bugsy? Sorry to spoil your Sunday afternoon, but we've got another dead choir member. It's at the garden centre where Aled was performing with them this afternoon.'

'Blimey!' Bugsy wiped his hands on the nearest rag, which was actually his wife Iris's silk scarf that had slipped off her lap when she got out of the car. 'Somebody must have it in for that lot. I wonder why. I mean, their singing can't be that bad. I'll summon up Big Ron and her body snatchers. She won't be happy. She goes to her Taekwondo class on Sunday afternoons.'

'Can you mobilize Norman's uniform lads to secure the crime scene?' said Jack. 'Aled's there on his own at the moment. He needs backup.'

'Yep. I'm on it, guv.'

Jack's phone rang again. This time the ringtone was 'Food, Glorious Food'. It was then he remembered that Corrie was at the garden centre with Cynthia Garwood. 'Hello, Corrie. Are you OK?'

'Yes, I'm fine, Jack, but I have a very traumatized elderly lady who has just found one of her fellow choir members dead in a shed. She won't let me call an ambulance for her because she says she's working undercover with Detective Williams and he'll need her to help take the statements. I told her there'll be other police officers who can do that, but there's no shifting her.'

'OK, get her a cup of tea and I'll be right there.'

Somehow, the news filtered through that there might be a killer on the loose in the garden centre and there was a mass exodus. People gathered up their children, grabbed their plants and legged it before someone tried to stop them. Most of the choir members stayed behind in the cafeteria at Aled's request, as did the garden centre staff, after he explained he was a police detective, but by the time uniform arrived, there were very few members of the public and the car park was virtually empty. Police tape was festooned over the whole of the outside yard and the pathologist and her team were examining the body and surrounding area.

'What have you got for us, Doc?' asked Bugsy. 'Cause of death looks fairly obvious.'

Dr Hardacre got up off her knees where she had been examining the wound. 'If deaths were obvious, Sergeant, you wouldn't need me.' She indicated the body. 'This poor lad didn't stand a chance. His attacker would have been standing in front of him and stabbed him once, right to the heart, but I don't believe he saw it coming. At least, he certainly wasn't expecting it. No defence wounds to his hands and no sign of a struggle. Just slash . . .' She jabbed at Bugsy's chest with stiff fingers and he staggered back slightly. 'The victim fell backwards through the door of the shed, which I understand had been left open to allow customers to see inside. Then the killer simply folded his legs in after him, shut the door and walked away.'

'That kind of suggests that he knew his attacker,' suggested Jack, 'and wasn't expecting violence. If he'd been approached threateningly, he'd have been on his guard and there'd have been a scuffle.'

'Very possibly,' agreed Dr Hardacre.

'How long has he been dead, Doctor?'

'About an hour, two at the most. You'll be wanting to know what weapon was used. At the moment, I can only suggest something very sharp with long thin blades — like a pair of scissors or shears. I'll know more when I get him on the slab. Post-mortem tomorrow morning, eight o'clock sharp, please.' She shouted to the mortuary attendants who were waiting inside. 'Right, you can take him away now, but not through the store. Take him through that side exit, please.' She indicated the double gates where the heavier stock was delivered and dispatched from trucks.

'Do you reckon that's how our killer escaped, guv?' asked Bugsy.

Jack thought about it. 'That's assuming he or she did escape and didn't just shove the body in the shed then go back inside and mingle with the other shoppers.'

'Bit risky, guv. Someone might have come out here to look at a bird bath or a greenhouse or something, while the killer was at it.'

'That's a risk they'd have had to take. I don't reckon this was premeditated. My instinct tells me that Luke was stabbed on the spur of the moment. A spontaneous decision by someone who hadn't come here expecting to commit murder. After all, it's not the ideal location, with crowds milling about and a choir concert going on that Luke was involved in, so he would be missed very quickly. Let's go and talk to the other members of the choir. We need to know who was the last to see him alive and when.'

They were about to go inside when one of the SOCOs shouted from the end of the yard. 'Sir, you need to see this. I think I've found the murder weapon.' He held up a pair of long, thin pruning scissors with yellow handles, still dripping water from where he'd found them amongst the weed at the bottom of the ornamental pond.

* * *

'Inspector Dawes, what's going on? Why are we being kept here? The coach is waiting to take us back to town.' Bryn Thomas, even more pompous than usual, strutted forward demanding answers.

'Please sit down, Mr Thomas, and I'll explain.' Jack thought not for the first time what an insufferable man he was. 'I'm very sorry to have to tell you that we have found the body of a young man who we believe to be a member of your choir.' Normally, Jack would have notified the next of kin first, but according to Aled, Geoff Smart reckoned Luke didn't have one. Tomorrow, he would ask Clive to delve into any information he could find, in case there was a distant relative somewhere who would want to take responsibility.

'Noooo!' The wail came from Ellie Bishop, who had made the obvious connection. 'It can't be Luke. He'd just gone to meet a friend, that's all. It isn't Luke! You're making a mistake.' She suddenly started gasping for breath and sank to her knees.

'Quick, where's her bag?' Dr Amory sprang into action. 'She's having an asthma attack. She needs her inhaler.'

Everyone scrabbled around looking for Ellie's backpack while she became progressively worse. Jack was taking no chances as she was wheezing and her lips were turning blue. He called for an ambulance.

'Dear God, Jack, whatever next?' Corrie appeared at his elbow. 'Cyn and I came here for a quiet afternoon, drinking pink cocktails and listening to the music. So far, there's been one bloody murder, an elderly lady whose blood pressure has probably dropped to terrifying depths from shock and a young girl fighting for breath. There are horror films on Netflix that are less harrowing.'

'I know, sweetheart. I don't know who's trying to put a stop to this choir, but I'm going to find out. Hopefully before they get a chance to take out anyone else. The CCTV should tell us something. I'm going to have a word with the manager.'

The ambulance arrived then and Ellie was stretchered away, still moaning Luke's name in between gasps. Her parents had been called and were on their way to the hospital.

The manager of the garden centre instructed the café staff to provide hot sweet tea to everyone. People were stunned and sat around, trying to take it in. There were still muted mutterings about the possible existence of a deranged serial killer, picking people off at random.

Jack took the manager to one side. 'Just a couple of requests, please. We shall need the CCTV that covers your outside yard — the shed area in particular.'

'Aah.' The manager shook his head. 'There aren't any cameras in that area, Inspector. You see, our CCTV is targeted at shoplifters. They take the smaller tools and plants that can be concealed in shopping bags and pushchairs, so we don't have cameras in the yard where the big items are displayed. I mean, you aren't going to see someone making off with a six-foot concrete statue of the Venus de Milo under his arm, are you?'

'No, I suppose not.' Jack had been hoping for a reasonable image of the killer. It seemed that he or she had been very lucky, especially as it appeared to be a spontaneous murder, so they may not have had time to assess the location of any cameras. 'Is it possible to have the CCTV footage covering the inside of the store, please?' Jack thought there was a slim chance they might see Luke going into the yard accompanied by someone. It wouldn't prove anything, but it would be a start.

'Yes, of course. This is a terrible thing, Inspector. We've never had anything like this happen here before. How is the elderly lady who discovered the . . . er . . . crime? She looked very shaken.'

'She's being looked after, thank you, sir. In my experience, elderly ladies are a lot tougher than they appear. It's the strong, macho men who tend to keel over at the sight of a body covered in blood.'

As if in confirmation, the manager blanched. 'Have you finished with me, Inspector? I think I could do with a cup of tea.'

Meanwhile, Geoff Smart had sought out Aled. 'What's going on, mate? Were the police expecting trouble? Is that why you joined the choir?'

'No. I was just doing a bit of investigation into the death of Charlie Snell. We certainly had no idea that this was going to happen.'

'Is there some maniac out there, picking us off one by one?' demanded Bryn. Unlike the other choir members who had changed out of the red tee-shirts into their own clothes, he was still wafting about in his long embroidered robe like Abanazar looking for a lamp to rub.

'Is there someone with a grudge against the choir?' suggested Jim.

'Who's going to be next?' wailed one of the young sopranos.

'Well, I'm not bloody volunteering!' exclaimed Roxy. 'Can we all go home now, Inspector Dawes? This place is giving me the creeps.'

Jack decided there was little to be gained in keeping people hanging about. 'If you would all please give your details to one of the uniformed officers, then you are free to go. Full statements can be taken at a later date. I shall want to know everybody's whereabouts throughout the tea break.'

'Jack, what about Mrs Dibble?' asked Corrie. 'I don't think she should be bundled onto a coach after what she's been through. Goodness knows what it's done to her internal workings.'

'Quite right. Aled, arrange for her to have a ride home in a police car, please, and ask one of the constables to see her safely into her house.'

* * *

It was too late to start cooking by the time Jack and Corrie finally arrived home, so supper was a paella from the freezer and a very large glass of wine.

Corrie sighed. 'So much for my afternoon off. There we were, Cyn and me, minding our own business, sipping our pink summer wine and admiring Aled's muscles, when suddenly, the place was full of coppers plodding about in their size twelves and putting the wind up everyone. Like I said, it would have been more relaxing if we'd stayed at home and watched *The Exorcist*.'

'Never mind that,' countered Jack. 'I missed the end of the rugby, Big Ron missed her Taekwondo class and Bugsy didn't finish mending his grandson's bicycle. The poor lad will probably go flying next time he rides it.'

'Murderers really should be more considerate about timing and only kill people during working hours,' said Corrie sarcastically. 'How awful, though. That poor young man. Violet Dibble said he had just been left there, bleeding, in the shed. Who would want to kill him?'

Jack shrugged. 'That's what I have to find out. The garden centre manager said Luke was very pleasant to the customers and a really good worker, got on well with his colleagues. Everybody liked him.'

'Well, somebody didn't.' Corrie produced a chocolate mousse from the fridge.

'Aled says the choir members now believe someone has it in for them and they're going to be picked off, one at a time. That's all I need — a diverse bunch of paranoid singers all looking over their shoulders and too scared to talk.' Jack helped himself to mousse. 'Is there cream to go with this?'

'Certainly not. Think of your cholesterol.' She was thoughtful. 'It certainly seems random, though. I mean, Charlie Snell was universally disliked, a middle-aged predator and rotten to his poor wife. Luke Burton was young, popular and madly in love with Ellie. They couldn't be less alike. All they had in common was the choir, so maybe the others are right to be on their guard.'

Jack nodded. 'Of course, I can't discount the theory that it could be someone from inside the choir, although the motive is hard to imagine.'

Corrie became animated. She clasped her hands. 'Now that Aled has been exposed as a police officer, you don't have a mole in the choir to observe the shifting conflicts, passions and betrayals that are seething in their breasts.'

Jack passed a weary hand over his eyes. 'Corrie, this is the Richington Community Choir we're talking about, not *Game of Thrones*. I doubt very much if those kinds of emotions are seething in anybody's breast. I wouldn't be surprised if half of them only turn out for the tea, buns and gossip.'

'Exactly!' yelped Corrie. 'I bet that choir is a hotbed of sin and depravity and the clues would be in the underground gossip.'

Jack was starting to detect a worryingly familiar turn in the conversation. 'You're not thinking of interfering by applying to join the choir, are you, Corrie? You can't sing — not even in the shower.'

'I know that. But I could offer to provide the tea and buns as Coriander's Cuisine's contribution to whatever charity they're supporting. I could keep my eyes and ears open and report to you anything that gives us a clue about any potential suspects.'

'Corrie, there's no "us" about it. Me detective — you caterer! It's much safer that way. Please stay out of it.'

She pulled a face. 'OK. If that's the way you want it. But you're missing a very good opportunity here.'

CHAPTER SEVEN

First thing on Monday morning, Detective Superintendent Garwood strode into the incident room and stood for some moments, frowning at the information on the whiteboard. 'Where is Inspector Dawes?' he asked the room in general.

'He's been slightly delayed by the traffic, sir,' answered Gemma cautiously. She had no idea where the inspector was, but she knew better than to say so.

'Well, I didn't have any trouble with traffic,' declared Garwood. 'No doubt he just overslept and . . . oh, there you are, Dawes.'

Jack, hearing Garwood's voice, had slipped in behind him, having discarded his coat outside in the corridor. 'Sorry, sir, were you looking for me?'

'Yes, Dawes. On my return from a very important conference in Harrogate, I find that two members of the Richington Community Choir have been murdered. First, a local butcher, and then yesterday, Mrs Garwood tells me there was another death at the very venue that she was attending with your wife. What's going on, Dawes, and what are you doing about it?'

'Well, sir, the team is following a number of leads, and . . .'

'Don't give me that public relations bollocks, man. You forget, I wrote most of it myself and I know bullshit when I hear it. What I want to know is, how close are you to catching the killer?'

In the absence of a lifeline, Jack trod water. 'We have followed normal procedures in a murder case like this, sir, and checked where all the choir members were at the time. Following interviews with everyone present, we can be reasonably sure they are all securely alibied, but as a senior detective of your considerable experience will know, there are inevitable obstacles when a murder is committed in a public place. SOCOs have reported multiple fingerprints, footfall and DNA. I'm about to attend the post-mortem of yesterday's victim and hopefully we'll know more after that.'

'Well, get on with it, man. I should point out that my Lodge supports the Community Choir and the various charities to which it is affiliated, so we need a swift result. Look for someone with a grudge, Dawes, before another of them cops it. Keep me informed.' He strode back to his office.

'The old man's in a bad mood this morning,' observed Bugsy caustically. 'Probably still hung-over.'

'He'll be in an even worse mood when he sees today's *Echo*, Sarge.' Aled passed it over.

The headline screamed:

*SERIAL KILLER AT LARGE
IN KINGS RICHINGTON. TWO DEAD
AND POLICE BAFFLED.*

'That's rubbish and totally inaccurate!' exclaimed Jack. 'For a start, there have to be at least three deaths for the murderer to be considered a serial killer, and we don't even know yet that it's the same person who's responsible. Who writes this nonsense?'

'The editor usually writes the headline and he's always had it in for the old man since the apocryphal golf match. He's more interested in sensationalism than substance. It's what sells papers and gets it on social media.' Bugsy looked at his watch. 'I think we should get over to the mortuary, guv. You know how tetchy Big Ron gets if we're late for a post-mortem.'

On the way out, Jack stopped to have a few words with Sergeant Parsloe. 'Norman, you know all the nutters in the area. Does anyone stand out as likely to do this?'

He shook his head. 'This is a community, Jack. One goes barmy, they all go barmy. That's what community does to people.'

* * *

Once more, the cold, clammy atmosphere of the examination room caught in Jack's throat and made him queasy. He fought it off and popped a mint in his mouth.

Dr Hardacre, grim and inscrutable behind the face mask, went through the usual preliminaries. 'Age early twenties, non-smoker, healthy and well-nourished. No signs of alcohol or drug abuse, but I'll know better when the tox report comes back. Death was caused by the penetration of a large blood vessel resulting in haemorrhagic shock. The poor lad would have lost consciousness almost immediately and bled out in minutes.' She held out a hand and Miss Catwater dutifully placed a sterile dish in it, containing the yellow-handled pruning scissors found at the bottom of the pond. 'I have compared this to the wound and I can confirm it is definitely the murder weapon, and before you ask, there were no fingerprints nor DNA. The scissors must have been wiped clean before the killer threw them in. That, and the effect of the chemicals they put in to clean the pond water, has made them virtually sterile. However, I did manage to identify minute traces of what has proved to be the victim's blood in the hinges. Equally, never discount the possibility that the killer might have worn gloves.'

'Did the SOCOs find Luke's phone?' asked Jack. He remembered that according to Aled, Ellie said she'd tried to phone him when he didn't turn up for his solo, but his phone was switched off.

Dr Hardacre shook her head. 'No, we didn't find a phone. Strange because most Gen Z individuals are virtually welded to their smartphones. I'm told they even have waterproof covers so they can take them into the shower. Of course, the killer might have taken it.'

Jack swore under his breath. 'Do you have anything at all that might help us, Doctor?'

'You may find this interesting, Inspector.' She held out her hand for another dish and this one contained the small corner of a photograph. 'I found this clutched in his closed fist. You're the detective, so make of it what you will, but in my opinion, he was holding the photograph and someone snatched it out of his hand, leaving behind just the torn corner. It's impossible to see an image, but I can tell you that the lab estimates the photo paper to be at least twenty years old.'

'Thank you, Doctor. If you find anything else, you'll let us know?'

'Of course.'

* * *

By the time they got back to the incident room, Clive, head of Digital Forensics, had information to report — or more accurately, the lack of it.

'The background check on Luke Burton is a little inconclusive, sir. He was adopted when he was only days old, but I couldn't find any trace of his original birth certificate, only his adoption certificate, so I can't tell if it was done legally. He had a very unsettled childhood, and for that reason, records are sparse, and some that I'd have expected to find are missing altogether. From what I could gather, his adoptive mother left home when he was little. I couldn't find a reason; she just vanished, probably abroad under a different name. His adoptive father died of alcohol poisoning soon after. Luke was taken into local authority care until he was old enough for the council to find him a flat then he got a job with the Richington Garden Centre. It was about then that he joined the choir, met Ellie and his life seems to have changed for the better.'

'That's a very sad start to life but an even sadder end, just as he'd found some happiness,' observed Velma.

'Some people don't have much luck, do they?' agreed Chippy. 'Makes me grateful that I grew up in a happy, loving home.'

'What I'm struggling with,' admitted Bugsy, 'is what motive the killer had. It almost certainly wasn't premeditated or planned, so why the sudden attack?'

'Not a spur-of-the-moment robbery — the poor guy wasn't carrying anything worth nicking,' observed Aled. 'I mean, you surely wouldn't fatally stab someone just to pinch their phone.'

'And it's unlikely it was some kind of disagreement that turned violent,' added Gemma. 'Everyone who knew him agreed that he was popular, pleasant and peace-loving.'

'Sir, I've had two of my officers watching the CCTV footage of the people inside the garden centre,' reported Clive. 'They spotted Luke going through the automatic doors to the outside yard during the tea break. He wasn't with anybody and nobody followed him out. At that stage, he was carrying a folder of some kind, but SOCOs didn't find it at the crime scene. The cameras lost him then and obviously he didn't return because he was lying dead in a shed.'

Gemma was looking at the photo of the murder weapon on the whiteboard. 'If Luke was killed by someone on impulse, they wouldn't have brought these pruning scissors with them to the garden centre in readiness, would they?'

'No, but where better to get hold of such an item than in a garden centre?' commented Chippy.

'Aren't garden retailers supposed to be extra vigilant about selling bladed items since the big increase in knife crime?' asked Velma. 'Couldn't we ask the manager for till receipts of everybody who bought this type of item? If we're really lucky, they will have used a credit card.'

'I don't think that will help,' offered Clive, 'because I don't think the killer bought them, just appropriated them. Take a look at this footage.' They gathered round. It showed a garden centre worker shaping a bay tree into a ball using pruning scissors with yellow handles, identical to the murder weapon. They watched as he put the scissors down when he was called away to speak to someone on one of the tills. When he came back, he looked around for them, but they had disappeared.

'Can you see who picked them up, Clive?' *At last a lead*, thought Jack.

'I'm afraid not, sir. The place was very crowded. It could have been anyone who walked past, hidden in amongst a mass of shoppers. I'll get my guys to take another look, but I don't hold out much hope.'

Jack felt as though he was taking two steps forward and three steps back. Now he had two murdered choir members and not a clue who killed either of them or why. In the case of Charlie Snell, there were too many suspects with a motive; in Luke's case, there didn't seem to be any. Might there be other suitors jealous of Luke's relationship with Ellie and who wanted him out of the picture? Then again, what if he was overthinking the whole thing? It wouldn't be the first time. It was a sad fact that in today's society, it wasn't unusual for a young person to take a knife to another on impulse and for the most trivial of reasons. But not here in Kings Richington, surely? Not here on his patch.

'What about Luke's phone?' asked Aled. 'I know SOCOs didn't find it, but he must have had one because, if you remember, Ellie Bishop tried to call him when he didn't turn up for his solo. She said it was turned off. If we found it, we could trace his last calls.'

'Good thinking, son,' said Bugsy. 'The killer might have phoned him to lure him outside to the yard. Could you do anything with that, Clive?'

'Do we know his number or which network he was with?' Clive replied.

'No, but we could ask Ellie,' said Jack. 'We need to speak to her as it seems he told her he was going to meet a friend. Aled, you and I have to find out what else he told her. In the meantime, can we get somebody over to Luke's flat, please? We need to search it for his laptop amongst other things.'

* * *

Ellie had been discharged from the hospital, but her parents were very protective when Jack and Aled turned up, wanting to speak to her.

'She's had a terrible shock, officers,' Mrs Bishop emphasized, 'and it triggered a very nasty asthma attack. Please be careful.'

'Of course, Mrs Bishop,' Jack assured her. 'It's just that she may have some information that will help us find Luke's killer.'

'What a dreadful business.' Mr Bishop shook his head sadly. 'What kind of world are we living in where a decent, hard-working young lad can have his life snuffed out by some random lout?'

'Rest assured, Mr Bishop, we shall catch whoever did this.' Jack sounded more confident than he felt.

'How can I help?' Ellie appeared in the doorway. She was pale and drawn and obviously very unhappy. 'I really want to help.'

'Of course you do, darling.' Her mother settled her on the sofa with cushions and a throw.

Jack sat beside her. 'I know this is painful, Ellie. You've lost a dear friend and we need to find out who's responsible. According to DC Williams here, you told Mr Thomas that Luke had gone to meet a friend when he didn't turn up for his solo. Was that all he told you?'

'Well, no.' She thought hard, trying to remember every detail. 'He said he was going to meet a friend during the tea break, but he didn't tell me who or where. He said it wouldn't take long, and he'd be back in good time for his solo. He was really buzzing and said he'd had some wonderful news, something that would change his life forever.'

'Did you have any idea what he meant?' asked Aled gently.

'No. He promised he'd explain later, when we were alone. But then you came and told us he was dead, so he couldn't. And now I'll never know what it was that made him so happy.' Her eyes filled with tears.

'You tried to phone him, but his mobile was switched off?' Jack asked gently.

'Yes, that's right. The Maestro was in a right strop. He said Luke going missing had ruined his running order.'

'Ellie, we think Luke's killer might have taken his phone. Could you give us the number you tried to ring, please?'

She gulped. 'Yes.' She reeled off the number. 'What if I ring it now? Do you think the murderer will answer?'

Jack shook his head. 'I very much doubt it, but it might give us a clue as to where the phone is located. Go ahead.'

Tentatively, she pulled her phone from her pocket, pressed Luke's number and passed it to Aled. He listened, then passed it to Jack. 'It's no use, sir. The message says *Not in Service.*'

They thanked her, then Jack decided they should leave as Ellie was starting to wheeze. On the way out, he turned back. 'Just one last question — when we found Luke, he had the torn corner of a photo in his closed fist. Did he show a photo to you?'

She nodded, remembering. 'Yes, he did. It was a faded picture of a young girl about my age, holding a baby in a shawl. I asked who it was, and he said he'd tell me later. I thought it was weird because he said he didn't have any family.'

* * *

Back at the station, Jack asked Clive if he could find out anything from the information they'd obtained. He was doubtful.

'*Not in Service* almost certainly means that whoever took Luke's phone has destroyed it and the number will have been disconnected.'

'What — like dropping it in the river?' asked Bugsy.

'No, Sarge. I mean really destroyed. Obliterated it entirely — case, hardware, SIM, the lot. It won't even go to voicemail.'

'How would you do that, Clive?'

'Hit it with a sledgehammer, grind it to bits, set fire to it — there are lots of ways. Now that I know the service provider, I'll see if they can help, but don't hold your breath.'

'Sir, I have Mrs Snell on the phone,' Gemma called out. 'She wants to speak to you.' She transferred the call across to him.

Jack picked up his phone, wondering how Mrs Snell was coping. Her life may not have been ideal before, but now it had been turned completely upside down. 'Hello, Mrs Snell. I'm very sorry, but I'm afraid we can't release your husband's body just yet, because . . .'

She interrupted. 'That isn't what I'm ringing about, Inspector Dawes. I've found something that I need you to see. Could you possibly come to the shop? It's important, otherwise I wouldn't bother you.'

Her voice sounded scared and Jack wondered what was causing it. He decided it was serious enough to go straight away. It might just be a step towards finding Snell's killer. They had precious little to go on so far. 'Yes, of course, Mrs Snell. We'll be there in half an hour.'

* * *

Bradley Snell was still home from university, and he unlocked the shop door to let Jack and Bugsy in. 'Thanks for coming so quickly, only Mum's been in a bit of a state since she found it.'

Doreen Snell came down from the flat above. She was flushed and her hair was dishevelled. No pleasantries or offers of tea and biscuits — straight to the matter in hand. 'Will you come outside to the garden shed, please?'

They all trooped outside and crammed into the shed. On the ground were the remains of a strong box, although it wasn't very strong now, as Bradley had smashed it open with a sledgehammer. Inside were bundles of twenty-pound notes and a number of passports.

'Only Charlie had the key to this box, Inspector.' Doreen was anxious to make it clear. 'I didn't even know it was there until Bradley came out here to get the lawnmower to tidy our bit of garden. He found it, hidden under a pile of sacks. I don't understand. What was Charlie doing with all those passports?'

'They're all expired,' added Bradley. 'Mum says she recognizes some of the names as customers who came into the shop asking to see my father but left without buying anything.'

Doreen Snell was clearly anxious to be rid of it. 'Will you take it all away, please, Inspector? I don't know what Charlie was up to, but Bradley and I don't want any part of it.'

'Yes, of course, Mrs Snell, but Forensics will want to examine these passports, so we may need to take yours and Bradley's fingerprints down at the station to eliminate you from our enquiries.' Bugsy pulled on the latex gloves that he always carried in his pocket and carefully picked up the cash and passports. 'Thank you for reporting this and please don't worry. We'll take it from here.'

Outside in the car, he bundled them into an evidence bag from the glove compartment. 'Another one of Snell's side hustles, guv? Norman was telling me that there's a fake passport scam thriving in the area and top brass are keen to crack it. These could be a part of it. Nice little earner for Charlie, though. No wonder he could afford all the big-brand gear.'

Jack was thoughtful. 'It looks like Snell was using the butcher's shop as a front to buy passports and sell them on. Probably to the men Aled photographed in the pub. Jim Scuttle has promised to let us know if they come in again.'

'Do you reckon it had something to do with why he was murdered?' asked Bugsy.

'It's too early to say, but it wouldn't surprise me.' Jack started the car.

* * *

Roxy Wild closed the shop early. It was unusual for her to be home by four o'clock, and by ten past, she was already halfway down a bottle of wine. She was on edge and had been for some time. Now the anxiety was really eating away at her. She feared she may have come across as a bit shifty when those two lady coppers had questioned her. Who was she kidding? She'd sounded dodgy even to her own ears, never mind theirs, and they were trained to pick up on anything false. She was sure the serious one with glasses had been suspicious, but at the time, she hadn't thought that what she'd told them — or to be accurate, what she *hadn't* told them — mattered all that much. But now poor Luke had been murdered, it was a whole new ball game. She poured another generous glass of Sauvignon Blanc and took a good swig. The question was — what to do next. She'd known Charlie had been up to something nasty — when hadn't he been? — but you don't point the finger unless you've got proof, and she hadn't. All she had of any substance was when two blokes had come into her shop, talking to each other in a language that she took to be Eastern European of some kind. One of them walked around, leering and fingering the knickers. The other came to the counter, chewing gum and looking her up and down. It was obvious that he hadn't come to buy some sexy lingerie for his wife when he asked if she could give them directions to Charlie's Chop Shop. She'd directed them to the butcher's shop down the high street. After they'd shambled out, she'd thought no more about it except that she was glad to see the back of them.

The worst part came when she'd gone round to Smart's Autos to speak to Geoff about her car, which was making a grating noise when she changed gear. She'd been about to go into the garage when she heard angry voices. Geoff and

Charlie were having a row. What she heard had unnerved her. Then there was the sound of a punch being landed and a scuffle with things breaking and lots of grunting and cursing. She'd jumped in her car, ignoring the gears' funny noises, and sped off down the bypass. After they'd all heard that Charlie had been murdered, she hadn't said anything because she and Geoff had been friends — and more — for years and she didn't seriously believe he was capable of killing anyone. Now Luke had been killed too, but she knew it couldn't have been Geoff because he'd been sitting in plain sight throughout the tea break. She decided that the best thing was to keep quiet. At least for the time being. After all, there was nothing to suggest that the same killer was responsible for both murders, was there? In any case, that nice young Detective Constable Williams was in the choir now, and if push came to shove, she'd have a word with him. She relaxed and went to fetch another bottle of wine.

CHAPTER EIGHT

With two choir members murdered, Felicity Thomas was drafting the weekly message for the blog. She had typed the glib 'our thoughts and prayers are with the families of our fellow choristers', although she knew this was hardly apt in either case but for different reasons. The last weeks had been hugely traumatic for her and she was finding it almost impossible to maintain her usual capable image. *Good old Fliss, always organized, never forgets anything and ready to produce tea and buns at the drop of a hat.* But she wasn't that person — not anymore — and she wondered how long she could keep up the facade. She was proposing to notify existing choir members and followers of the blog that the Richington Community Choir would cease to perform, at least for the foreseeable future. She was checking it for accuracy before she posted it when she became aware that Bryn had crept up behind her and was reading over her shoulder.

'What do you think you're doing, you stupid woman!'

She took a deep breath and resisted what was now the almost constant urge to pick up something heavy and hit him with it, and keep on hitting him until he shut up — for good. 'The choir can't continue after what's happened, Bryn. You must see that.'

'I see nothing of the sort. There is no reason why the choir shouldn't carry on as normal.' He flicked back his hair in a gesture of waning dominance, like an old lion shaking a greying and sparse mane as the hyenas closed in.

'Shouldn't we at least check with the police that it's OK to continue while their investigations are ongoing?' Fliss asked, weary of these confrontations.

'Absolutely not. They didn't see fit to consult me before parachuting a detective into the choir, and what good did he do? Another choir member was murdered right under his nose. No, we shall soldier on, Felicity. What you should be posting is a reminder that there's a practice tonight in the room above the Richington Arms. And when you've done that, I want you to post an advertisement for a basso-profundo and a counter-tenor to apply for an audition. We are missing voices at both ends of the scale which need to be replaced, or the balance of sound will be lost. Get on with it and stop questioning my authority.' He strode out.

Even as she typed, Felicity could feel the overwhelming resentment burning inside her. She knew her friends couldn't understand why she didn't just leave Bryn, but she couldn't. The Edwardian house, the home she'd grown up in, had been passed down to her by her parents after they died, together with a generous sum of money. They believed it would give her security and independence and so it had, until she married Bryn, the classic narcissist. When they first met, he had seemed charming, persuasive and worldly. She had been a naive primary school teacher, several years younger, and impressed by his knowledge of music and composers. In those early days, he had taken her to concerts and she had been completely under his spell. His clothes were colourful and unconventional and he wore his hair long, which in those days was considered avant-garde and extrovert. But once they were married, he had persuaded her that it would be better 'for tax reasons' if the house was in his name and their money transferred into a joint account — *her money* in reality as he didn't have any, only his meagre wages which he spent on goodness knows what. It was only after he had effectively taken control of her home, her money and her life that he began to treat her with disdain, belittling her in front of everyone, telling her she was mentally disturbed and assuring her that she had to stay with him because nobody else would want her. If she left him, he said, the courts would undoubtedly decide in his favour when it came to apportioning their assets — *her* assets! What did they call mental cruelty these days? Coercive control? Gaslighting? Well, she'd show him!

* * *

A mile out of town in the elegantly furnished study of Richington Court, Julian Amory was sitting at his eighteenth-century Hepplewhite desk trying to make sense of the spreadsheet on his laptop. His company had done rather well out of the pandemic, buying from the manufacturers who were making cheap protective equipment then selling it at a massive mark-up. But since then, a combination of market instability, insufficient cash flow and fluctuating economics meant it had suffered a sharp downturn in profitability. He conceded that his gambling habit may also have had something to do with it. Whichever way he cut it, the bottom line was that this extravagant and very lavish house would have to go. The running costs alone were exorbitant never mind the second mortgage he'd taken out, the payments of which seemed to double with every Bank of England announcement. He went to the drinks cabinet and poured himself a generous single malt. That was something else that he'd no longer be able to afford. His immediate problem was how he would explain it to Elizabeth. She had her sights set on becoming the next mayor and, soon after that, a Member of Parliament. He couldn't imagine her understanding when he told her they would have to downsize to a rented house on a council estate somewhere in town. Added to which, there was a very real risk that his unorthodox business dealings would come to light, and having a husband prosecuted for fraud wouldn't fit with her aspirations to be an MP of integrity and rectitude at Westminster. He poured himself the last of the whisky. He was meant to be at a board meeting in an hour. He'd have to ring for a taxi if he didn't want to be done for drink-driving on top of everything else.

'Are you still here?' Elizabeth Amory burst in, looking for her car keys.

'No, my love, I left half an hour ago. What you see here is a cardboard replica.'

'Don't try to be clever, Julian, it doesn't suit you.' She bustled about, looking under papers and in pin trays. 'Have you seen my car keys? I'm supposed to be chairing a Soroptimist meeting in Richington Town Hall. We're targeting the glass ceiling in the workplace and how to smash through it.' It may have been a trying week that she wouldn't want to repeat, she'd decided, but life had to go on — otherwise, what was the point of it all?

Secretly, Julian reckoned Elizabeth could smash through any glass ceiling using just her tongue, but he didn't say so. 'The last time I saw your keys, they were in the pantry, on top of the quinoa. You were making kale and quinoa burgers.'

'Oh yes, I remember. They were delicious.'

'They were grotesque.'

'Really, Julian, in a high-powered, stressful job like yours, one would have thought you'd appreciate the benefits of a diet that lowers your chances of a heart attack and colon cancer. And sitting there drinking whisky is hardly going to earn you the knighthood that we need, is it?'

'No, dear.'

She hurried out to fetch her keys from the pantry.

And since, he pondered, *I'm unlikely to have that high-powered, stressful job for much longer, let alone a knighthood, I have every intention of going to my club for chateaubriand steak and chips after the board meeting. I shall enjoy it while I still can.*

* * *

Jack and Bugsy had been out to Richington Forest to have another look at the site where Charlie Snell had been killed. It still bore the remnants of police tape flapping in the wind around the trees and the bare patch where Snell had fallen. SOCOs had combed through almost every blade of grass and piece of forest litter. With Garwood leaning on Jack virtually every day for a result, they had hoped to find something that would at least provide a clue.

Bugsy scratched around for a bit then gave up. 'It's no good, guv, Big Ron's team would have found something if it had been here to find. Either by luck or cunning, the killer has managed to pull off an almost perfect murder — aided by the weather, of course.'

'Which makes me wonder,' said Jack thoughtfully, 'whether they've done it before. You know what Saint Agatha of Christie said about murder being easy . . . .'

'I didn't have you down as a reader of murder mysteries, guv.' Bugsy was surprised. 'I thought you'd have had enough of it during the day.'

'I'm not as a rule, but I fell asleep watching Sports Night on the TV and woke up wondering why the lady rugby pundit had turned into Miss Marple. Once I started watching, I had to carry on until I found out whodunnit.'

'Course you did, guv. Force of habit.' Bugsy grinned to himself.

As they drove back, they approached several large factories on the bypass. 'That's the company where Bryn Thomas claims he's a top executive in retail distribution,' said Bugsy. 'Weren't we going to find out why he's only on minimum wage and whether he declared his conviction for ABH?'

'Good thinking.' Jack drove into the car park, avoiding the spaces with name plates marked out for senior management. He looked for a space with Bryn's name on it but couldn't see one. Once inside, they showed their warrants to the receptionist behind the desk in the opulent foyer and asked to speak to the manager responsible for retail distribution. She motioned to them to take one of the plush and very expensive seats and picked up the phone. While they waited, subdued music played in the background and the large screen on the wall showed a video of the products and their global distribution. 'This is a thriving international company,' Jack murmured to Bugsy. 'Thomas has done well to have secured a managerial position here.'

'Which brings up the question of whether he declared his prison record when he applied.' Bugsy doubted it.

A few minutes later, a man of about thirty wearing a Savile Row suit and handmade shoes emerged from the lift. 'Good afternoon, officers, I'm Peregrine Lloyd-Robinson — Perry to my friends.' He smiled genially. 'I understand you want to talk to me.' He shook their hands. 'It isn't often we get a visit from the police.' He gave a wry smile. 'My wife hasn't parked the Bentley on a yellow line again, I hope. She says there are never enough parking spaces outside Harrods.'

Jack was puzzled. 'No, it's nothing like that, sir. We were hoping to speak with the retail distribution manager.'

'Yes, that's me. I have a team of clever executives who do the real work, of course. What's the name of the man you're looking for?'

'Bryn Thomas,' said Bugsy. 'Maybe he's one of your deputy managers.'

'No, sorry.' He looked blank. 'Doesn't ring any bells.' He spoke to the receptionist. 'Cressida, check the staff lists. Do we have anyone of that name working for us?'

She tapped a few keys. 'Yes, sir. Mr Thomas is in the warehouse.'

'There you go, officers. Our warehouse is in the basement. Down in the lift to your right.' He pointed. 'You must excuse me; I'm expecting an important call from Los Angeles. Please don't hesitate to let me know if I can help further.' He hurried back to his office suite.

Jack and Bugsy took the lift down to the basement and looked around. 'There he is, guv.' Bugsy spotted him. 'Over there, driving that forklift. He's got his hair tied back in a ponytail and his beard in a hairnet. Health and Safety, I expect, in case they get caught in the machinery. This is going to be an interesting conversation.'

When Thomas saw them, he looked around him guardedly, then parked his truck and climbed down. He called out to the foreman, 'I'm just going for my break.' He hurried across to Jack and Bugsy and chivvied them out into the corridor. 'What the hell are you doing here? You've no business harassing me like this! I shall make a formal complaint.'

'We aren't harassing you, Mr Thomas,' said Jack reasonably. 'We just want to ask you some questions. For example, why did you tell my detective constable you were a managing director when you're actually a forklift driver?'

'All right, so I embellished the truth a little. It isn't a crime, is it? And anyway, Williams wasn't exactly truthful when he didn't admit he was a police officer.'

'DC Williams was trying to uncover information about who murdered your basso-profundo and now Luke Burton. What was your reason for lying about your job?' Jack asked.

'It's about personal esteem, Inspector. I have a position to maintain in the community, and I'd be grateful if you kept what you have found out to yourselves. It has nothing whatsoever to do with the cases you're investigating and would be in breach of my . . . er . . . privacy — or something of that nature.'

'Fair enough, Mr Thomas. As far as we're concerned, you can pretend to be Batman in your personal life, but what is rather more serious is whether you declared your conviction and subsequent prison sentence for actual bodily harm when you applied for this job.'

Thomas's face went white, then pink, then red, then back to a ghostly pallor.

'You see, sir,' continued Bugsy, 'knowingly lying on your job application with the intention of securing employment is a criminal offence under the Fraud Act 2006, and on conviction, you could be sentenced to up to ten years inside.'

Thomas looked from Jack to Bugsy, his mouth opening and closing like a goldfish but with no sound coming out.

Eventually, he croaked, 'Please . . . I can't go back to prison . . .'

'The best thing you can do now, Mr Thomas, is to go along to the Human Resources Manager, confess you lied and hope all they do is fire you. We will check you've done it, of course. And if you remember anything about the deaths of Charlie Snell and Luke Burton, it's vital that you tell us. Do you understand?'

'Yes, officer. I will. I promise.'

* * *

It was about the same time that Aled decided to check on Violet Dibble. He knew elderly ladies were tougher than they appeared — everyone kept telling him so. All the same, it must have given her a terrible shock finding Luke lying in a pool of his own blood. Aled had been brought up to be a kind and compassionate young man and he felt he had a duty of care as, rightly or wrongly, Violet saw herself as his deputy.

She lived in a warden-controlled bungalow in the Sunny Homes Senior Village, a complex close to Richington Park. She welcomed him effusively. 'How lovely to see you, Agent Williams. And what good timing. I'm knitting you a sweater and now I shall be able to measure the length of your arms.' She bustled off to make tea. Aled looked around the small living room. There were framed photos of her late husband, Robert Dibble, and Pavarotti, the deceased cat, but no children or grandchildren. Coming from a large family, Aled thought that was sad. When she returned carrying a tea tray, he took it from her and put it on the table.

'How is the investigation coming along?' She poured tea and cut slices of raspberry sponge cake. 'Are you any closer to finding the killer before another one of us bites the dust?'

'Trust me, we're working on it, Mrs Dibble. But it's hard to imagine anyone with a motive for both Charlie Snell and Luke Burton. They were completely different men with opposite lifestyles.' He took a slice of cake from the plate she proffered. 'Can you think of anyone who might have a grudge against the choir as a whole?'

'Well, now that you mention it, have you questioned Camilla Hoskins?'

That was a name Aled hadn't heard back at the station and he was certain she wasn't on the whiteboard. 'No, we haven't. Who is she?'

'She was chief co-ordinator of MARC.'

'Pardon?' He wondered if he'd heard right.

'Mothers Against Richington's Choir. They caused a terrible fuss when the choir first started up. Wrote to the council, protested outside the church hall with banners when we were practising, and threw eggs at the cars. Bryn had to call the police a couple of times.'

'Surely the choir does a lot for the community and local charities. What were they protesting about?'

'They said that choir members parked their cars all over Richington Green and on the pavement. Mothers couldn't get their buggies past, the singing kept their babies awake and, of course, they couldn't take their dogs out to shit all over the Green. It was a load of rubbish. I think the real reason Camilla started it was because she auditioned for the choir and Bryn turned her down. He said her voice was a crime against music. If I remember rightly, he likened it to a cat with its tail shut in the door. She didn't like it.'

'I haven't seen any protests since I joined the choir,' said Aled.

'No, she lost public support when nothing happened to stop us. Camilla's a ghastly woman with a warped idea of what's important in life, but I don't believe she's capable of killing off members of the choir out of spite. Anyway, she's found a different crusade now. She co-ordinates WART — Women Against Richington's Traffic. They want the whole of Richington High Street pedestrianized so mothers can wheel their buggies all over the road and into people's shins with impunity and toddlers can run riot without having to be controlled. If it ever happens, I intend to buy one of those souped-up mobility scooters and I shall whizz down the street, prodding people out of the way with my stick.' She picked up the teapot. 'More tea, Detective?'

On the way back to the station, Aled couldn't help smiling to himself. He hoped he'd be as feisty and spirited as Violet when he was her age. He didn't think this Camilla whatsname was a credible suspect, but if all else failed, he'd have a word.

* * *

When Jack got home that evening, he found Corrie poring over unfamiliar food recipes involving crushed mutton, stewed goat and lots of exotic spices.

'Jack, what do you know about Richington Malworthy?'

'Not much. Only that it's a remote village on the southern boundary of Kings Richington. Why do you want to know?'

'I've had a request for what amounts to a rather fancy banquet on Friday night.'

'Is that causing you problems?' Jack began laying the table for supper, which he suspected might be his favourite corned beef hash, so he sneaked out the brown sauce. Corrie disapproved of bottled sauce.

'No, not really. It's just that it's outside my normal delivery limit, but I'm willing to give it a go. It's a good order — twenty covers.'

'OK, but watch yourself. Norman Parsloe calls it "bandit country" because it's on the border of two police divisions, so neither wants to take responsibility for it.'

'Oh great!' Corrie exclaimed. 'So it's a haven for crooks and criminals?'

'Something like that. They know they're unlikely to be spotted by an area car when they're joyriding or pushing drugs on street corners, but I don't think it's the hideout of escaped bank robbers and fugitives from justice. You don't need a pepper spray and a pit bull, but I'd take Carlene with you, though. She can ride shotgun through the Badlands.'

'Well, that's a comfort. I'll get Carlene to give you a ring if I'm sold into slavery or kidnapped and held to ransom.'

'OK, dear, but try not to get kidnapped while the rugby's on.'

CHAPTER NINE

It started out as a quiet Wednesday morning in the incident room. Clive and his team were trawling through hours of CCTV for any unusual activity. They had recordings from the garden centre, the street outside Charlie's Chop Shop, Wild Styles and as much footage as was available of the road leading to Richington Forest. Clive had contacted the service provider of Luke Burton's phone and they were still trying to locate some data, but it was proving difficult if not impossible. When Jack's phone rang, it was a welcome intrusion to the stalemate with at least a hope of progress. He snatched it up. It was Sergeant Parsloe.

'Hello, Norman. What can we do for you?'

Norman's voice was sombre, unlike his usual cheery banter. 'Jack, there's been another murder.'

Jack groaned. 'Please tell me it isn't another choir member or I'll start to think the editor of the *Echo*'s responsible, just to prove his claim that there's a serial killer on the loose.'

'I'm afraid it *is* another choir member, Jack.' He paused. 'It's Violet Dibble.'

Jack didn't speak for long moments, then asked, 'When? Where?'

'She was found earlier this morning in her bungalow, dead in her armchair.'

'Who found her?'

'It was Dr Amory, Jack. The poor woman is severely traumatized, apparently. Who wouldn't be? That's two dead bodies she's discovered in a matter of weeks. She must feel like the angel of death. The warden of the complex phoned it in. She has Dr Amory in her kitchen, drinking hot sweet tea for the shock. Dr Hardacre and her SOCOs are already on the scene.'

'I'm leaving now.' Jack put down the phone and grabbed his coat.

'Is that another murder, sir?' Aled called out. 'Do you need me to come and take statements?'

'No, thanks, Aled.' Jack decided it wouldn't be wise as he knew Aled had formed a special connection with Violet, albeit unintentionally.

DC Dinkley, who had an uncanny perception of people's unspoken thoughts, met Jack's eye and knew immediately who the victim was. She said nothing.

'I'll update the whole team when I know the details,' promised Jack. 'Please carry on with the background checks. Bugsy, you're with me.'

* * *

When Jack and Bugsy arrived at what Richington Council was pleased to call the Sunny Homes Senior Village, SOCO vans filled the small car park and a uniformed constable guarded the main entrance to prevent any visitors from just walking in. Inside, police tape secured the bungalow where Violet had lived for the last ten years. PC 'Johnny' Johnson had been the first uniformed police constable to attend after Sergeant Parsloe received the call. He stood outside the front door and lifted the tape for them to duck under. He looked pale.

'Are you OK, Constable?' Jack asked.

He swallowed hard. 'Yes, thank you, sir. Nasty business. Poor old lady. Who'd do a thing like that?'

'That's what we're going to find out, son,' replied Bugsy with conviction. 'We'll get him, don't you worry.'

Dr Hardacre was kneeling down beside the riser-recliner armchair where Violet sat, eyes closed, knitting on her lap, looking for all the world as if she was having a nap.

'What have we got, Doctor?' Jack asked.

Big Ron clambered to her feet, scowling. 'You will observe, gentlemen, that there is only one needle in the victim's knitting. The other has been pushed with considerable force into her ear.' She pointed.

'Are you serious, Doc?' asked Bugsy, appalled.

She glared at him. 'I don't do "funny", Sergeant. You should know that by now.'

Jack recoiled. 'What a terrible way to kill someone.'

'Did the needle go right into her brain?' asked Bugsy, unsure whether he wanted the details.

'It doesn't need to reach the brain in order to kill, Sergeant. The brain floats in cerebrospinal fluid, in a tissue sac within the skull. Somewhat like an egg in its shell. All you have to do is puncture that and let the fluid out. As the sac drains, the brain no longer floats and begins to compress the medulla oblongata. This causes death by disrupting cerebral regulation of breathing and heart rate. It wouldn't have taken long.'

Jack looked around at the immaculately tidy living room. China ladies in crinolines stood unmolested on the mantelpiece and bureau drawers were disturbed only by SOCOs in protective suits. He directed a questioning look at the officer going though Violet's handbag, which was down by the side of her chair. 'Anything missing?'

'This week's pension is intact in her purse, sir, and her bank cards are untouched.'

So not a robbery gone wrong then, thought Jack. In his experience, burglars who raided these types of homes robbed more than one house, quickly, then legged it as fast as they could. They didn't hang about killing people and they usually broke in at night. Theft was one thing — if you were caught, you got a few years inside. Murder — you got life.

'How long has she been dead, Doctor?'

'At a rough estimate, about two hours, so time of death around noon. You need to speak to Dr Amory, who found her. She's in the warden's kitchen. I'll let you have a report on anything the SOCOs find and whether the post-mortem throws up anything unexpected.'

'Thanks, Doc.' Bugsy was in need of tea himself, if not something stronger.

Jack took one last look at the sad, motionless body of Violet Dibble slumped in her chair, then they made their way across the complex to the warden's bungalow.

Elizabeth Amory was sitting at the kitchen table holding a mug in trembling hands. She jumped up when Jack came in the door. 'What's happening, Inspector Dawes? First Snell, then Luke and now Violet. It's as if the wrath of God has descended upon us. Who is carrying out this terrible vendetta against the choir?'

Jack patted her shoulder. 'Rest assured, we shall find out and put a stop to it.'

'Well, I believe you, but I'm not at all sure that the rest of the choir will. They were spooked already, before this happened.' She sank down on her chair again.

'Does Mrs Dibble have any relatives that you know of? Anyone we should notify?' asked Bugsy.

'No, I don't believe so. If you were thinking that some family member killed her off to inherit her money, I'm not even sure she had any — money or relatives.'

'Tell us about how you came to discover the body, please.' Bugsy had his notebook ready.

Dr Amory took off her glasses, closed her eyes and pinched the bridge of her nose. She needed to get this exactly right. 'I'd just popped round about half an hour ago to see how Violet was. That would have been about one thirty. I'd brought a vegan cheese and pickle sandwich for her lunch. I'm chief co-ordinator of FORE, you see.'

They looked blank.

'Friends Of Richington's Elderly. We're a group of community-minded volunteers who take it in turns to visit elderly folk who don't have any relatives. I knew Violet was shaken at finding poor Luke Burton's body, so I came here first. She isn't strong and these things take their toll. It's knocked some of the stuffing out of me, I don't mind admitting. I tapped on the door and called out, but she didn't answer, so I opened it and went in. She never locks it. At first, I just thought she'd dozed off, so I patted her on the arm and then I saw the needle.' She shuddered. 'I'm afraid I touched it briefly, wondering if I should try to pull it out. Stupid of me, of course, but I didn't stop to think.'

'No, I don't expect you did, Madam. Did you see anyone else in the vicinity? Anyone at all?' asked Bugsy.

'No. No one. As soon as I saw Violet was dead, I said a quick prayer. Then I ran here to the scheme manager's bungalow and she phoned your people.'

'Yes, that's right,' confirmed the warden. 'It's such a shock. Obviously people die here, it goes with the territory, but not like this. Do you know how much longer your forensic people will be, Inspector?'

'As long as it takes to complete their work,' he replied bluntly. 'We shall need your CCTV recordings.' Jack had seen the cameras on the way in.

The warden furrowed her brow, wondering how to explain. 'I'm afraid there aren't any. There are cameras, but they don't record anything. The residents objected.'

'But it's for their own safety,' protested Bugsy.

'Yes, but they didn't see it like that. They saw it as snooping. Big Brother stuff. They said it was only a matter of time before officials would want to snoop into their finances as well as their comings and goings and they weren't having it. They even started a petition to have the cameras disconnected, so the CCTV had to go.'

And with it, thought Jack wearily, *goes our only chance of seeing who went into Violet's bungalow this afternoon and murdered her.*

* * *

Bad news travels fast and by the time Jack and Bugsy got back to the station, the team already knew about Violet Dibble's death, and since communities love to gossip, so did most of Kings Richington. In the tight-knit community, the air was thick with whispers and hushed conversations. The choir, once a symbol of unity and joy, had become the centre of a chilling mystery. The recent murders of several choir members had sent shockwaves through the town, leaving everyone on edge and fuelling a frenzy of gossip.

When the first victim, Charlie Snell, was found in Richington Forest, a place usually filled with the harmonious sounds of birds and the breeze whispering in the trees, people were filled with disbelief. The discovery was gruesome, and the news had spread like wildfire. Speculations about the motive and the identity of the murderer ran rampant. Some believed it was an outsider, while others feared it was someone within their own ranks. The choir members, once seen as pillars of the community, were now viewed with suspicion and alarm. Fearing more bodies would be discovered, the gossip grew more intense. The local café became a hub for exchanging theories and rumours. Conversations were dominated by the latest developments, with each person adding their own twist to the story. Some claimed to have seen shadowy figures lurking around the church hall at night, while others swore they had heard eerie noises during choir rehearsals. The sense of paranoia was palpable, and trust among the townsfolk began to erode.

Jack's police investigation was ongoing, but the confusion and lack of concrete leads only fuelled the community's speculation. Every choir member's past was scrutinized, and secrets that had long been buried began to surface. Relationships were strained, and the once harmonious choir was now fractured by fear and mistrust. The murders had not only taken lives but had also shattered the sense of security and camaraderie that the choir had once brought to Kings Richington.

In the midst of the chaos, the community struggled to find solace. The church hall, a place of refuge and peace, now stood as a reminder of the horrors that had unfolded. The choir's music, which had once uplifted spirits, was now a haunting echo of the tragedies. As the gossip continued to swirl, the townsfolk were left grappling with the unsettling reality that the murderer could be among them, hiding in plain sight.

Down on the front desk, Sergeant Parsloe was fielding fractious enquiries about another member of the Richington Community Choir having been killed and what the police were doing about it. He was churning out the usual 'we're following a number of leads'.

'Aled, son, do you want to take a couple of hours off?' asked Bugsy. 'This must be particularly hard for you.'

'No, thanks, Sarge. I want to help catch the bastard who did this. Mrs Dibble thought she was working with me as my deputy and that makes me responsible.'

'No, it doesn't, Aled, but I understand that's how you feel,' said Jack. 'You could start by doing door-to-door enquiries at the Sunny Homes Village. One of the neighbours might have seen something while they were mowing the grass or hanging out the washing. It's worth a punt. Take Chippy with you.'

'Yes, sir.' They grabbed their jackets and hurried out.

'Gemma and Velma, can you get over to Luke Burton's flat and search for anything that might explain why he thought his life was taking a turn for the better? His laptop would be useful if we haven't already impounded it.'

'Sir,' they chorused.

'That was an interesting division of labour, guv,' observed Bugsy after they'd gone. 'Why did you send the lads to Sunny Homes and the girls to Luke's flat and not the other way around?'

'Elementary, my dear Bugsy,' replied Jack. 'Elderly ladies and gents living in assisted accommodation are more likely to open up to polite, tidy-looking young men while young ladies are better at ferreting out secret hiding places where we wouldn't think to look.'

'Blimey, Jack, you'd better not say that in public. The stereotype police, aka Gemma, would be down on you like a ton of bricks.'

* * *

Sunny Homes Retirement Village consisted of eleven bungalows — ten residents and one occupied by the scheme manager. Aled and Chippy took half each, either side of what had been Violet Dibble's home.

Aled knocked on the door of Violet's immediate neighbour, wondering if he should have taken the warden with him so the residents didn't feel threatened. He needn't have worried.

A gnarled, arthritic hand appeared around the edge of the chained-up door, followed by part of a whiskery face. 'Whatever you're selling, I don't want any. We're in mourning for a neighbour. Go away.' The door began to close.

'It's Mrs Dibble I'm here about, sir,' said Aled hastily. He didn't want to appear confrontational by putting his foot in the door. 'I'm a police officer.' He held up his warrant card. 'We're knocking on doors asking if anyone saw or heard anything suspicious around lunchtime.'

'Apart from my guts rumbling while I opened a tin of soup, no, I didn't.' He softened. 'Poor Vi. Who'd do a terrible thing like that? I mean, we're all getting on in these bungalows. Living on borrowed time, waiting to be called, you might say. But nobody wants to go like that.'

'No, sir. And we're doing our utmost to catch whoever's responsible.' Aled looked around. 'You can see the car park from your window. Did you see any unfamiliar cars coming and going?'

'What, you mean before all those police vans turned up and blocked my view? No, I didn't. Only Busy Lizzie's sports car. She's always poking her nose in. Reckons she's some kind of God-bothering social worker. She was here.'

'Yes, we know about her. It was Dr Amory who found Mrs Dibble. What time did she arrive?'

'Don't remember. I didn't take a lot of notice of her. Nobody does.'

'So you didn't see anybody loitering or hear any noise from next door?'

'No. I used to hear Vi singing in her garden sometimes, when she was pegging out her washing, but I never heard anything today.' He sniffed. 'I suppose she's pegged out for the last time now.' His rheumy eyes filled with tears. 'If there's nothing else, I need a pee.'

'Well, thank you for your time, sir. If you think of anything, please give me a call.' Aled pushed a card into his hand, not wanting to be responsible for an old gentleman wetting himself on his own doorstep. He felt guilty enough already.

Down the other end of the row of bungalows, DC Chippendale wasn't having any better luck. He had declined the offer of tea from at least three ladies and reassured one of them that a serial killer wasn't lying in wait to jump out at her when she went to bingo. Another asked if she would be safe as long as she didn't sing in the choir.

A retired train driver lived in the last bungalow. He opened the door when Chippy knocked, and when he realized he was a police officer, he stepped forward as if to shake hands and overbalanced on the step. Chippy grabbed his arm to steady him.

'Ow! Ow! That's assault, that is! It's police brutality.' He nursed his arm as if it was broken. 'That'll be worth at least a four-figure compo! Who do I complain to?'

Chippy wisely ignored this outburst. 'You will have heard about the death of Mrs Dibble in number three. I'm asking her neighbours if they know anything that might enable us to catch her killer, sir. Can you help at all?'

'No, but it wouldn't surprise me if it wasn't one of them council fat cats up the Town Hall who keep putting up the rent. That's who you want to be looking at, not honest, retired working men. I slogged on the trains for thirty years, when we wasn't on strike. Now I'm struggling to get by on a pension that wouldn't keep a squirrel in nuts. Don't talk to me about social equality. Bugger off!' He slammed the door.

Chippy came away with nothing new regarding the investigation but with a more fundamental view of the public he had pledged to serve.

* * *

Luke Burton's tiny flat was right at the top of a block within cycling distance of the garden centre where he worked. It was small but adequate for a young man on his own. The lift wasn't working, so Gemma and Velma climbed the stairs until they reached his door. It was locked.

'Did the Inspector give you the key?' asked Gemma.

'No,' replied Velma. 'I thought you had it.'

'Do you mean we've come all this way, climbed four flights of stairs and now we can't get in?'

Velma crouched down and peered at the lock. 'Have you got anything long and thin?'

Gemma rummaged in her bag. 'Will this do?' She produced a metal crochet hook.

Velma took it. 'Perfect.' She grinned. 'I didn't know you could crochet.'

'I can't,' admitted Gemma. 'It belongs to my gran. Back in my uni days, I was always locking myself out of my flat, so she gave it to me and I've carried it around ever since. She's an incredible lady. Her great-grandmother was a suffragette. She has a sepia photo of her in a silver frame.'

'That explains a lot,' muttered Velma. 'Aled says Mrs Dibble was an incredible lady. He's really cut up about her dying.'

'We have to find the maniac who's killing these people,' said Gemma vehemently. 'Otherwise, what good are we as police officers? I suppose you'll say we're not allowed to call people maniacs anymore.'

'Neurodiverse,' replied Velma. 'Or in this case, sociopathic.'

'Well, I don't care what you want to call this person; it doesn't give him an excuse to kill.' Gemma was emphatic. 'I've seen too many people get away with breaking the law because of the label some health professional had put on them.'

Velma knelt down by the door-knob, which had a small round hole in the centre to allow for emergency access. She shoved in the hook, pushed hard and wiggled it about. The door clicked open and they were in.

'How do you want to handle this?' asked Gemma.

'How about we split up and search the rooms individually, then swap over. That way we shouldn't miss anything.'

After half an hour of exploring every drawer, cupboard and appliance, they finally met up in the kitchen.

'Did you find Luke's laptop?' asked Velma.

'No. I don't think he had one,' decided Gemma. 'There's no sign of a charger, either.'

'Maybe he couldn't afford one. We know he had a mobile phone, but maybe garden centre wages didn't run to a laptop.'

'What do you make of this?' Gemma held out a library book entitled *The Characteristics of the Gene*. 'I found it on Luke's bedside table. He must have had it for a while because it's overdue.'

Velma opened it and thumbed through a few pages. 'It's about features that are inherited from your parents. Unusual reading for a young man of twenty-something without any parents. I think we should take it back to the library and pay the fine. Someone might remember Luke and be able to fill in a few blanks.'

Gemma chewed her lip. 'There are only photographs of Ellie pinned to the wall. I wonder why?'

'It's because, unlike your gran, Luke didn't have any distant relatives, not that he knew about, anyway.'

'So who was in the twenty-year-old photo that was torn out of his hand?' wondered Gemma. 'It couldn't have been Ellie. She's only seventeen.'

'And why would the killer take it?' Velma frowned. 'I'm starting to get strange vibes about these murders. Everyone's assuming the killer is someone with a pathological hatred of the choir and is picking them off at random. I'm not so sure. Why would anyone do that? I think there's a lot more to it that we haven't found out.'

* * *

The library was virtually empty when Gemma and Velma walked through the automatic door. Just a few intellectuals browsing amongst the Ethics and Philosophy section.

'What's that funny smell?' Velma wrinkled her nose.

'Wet anoraks and piccalilli,' replied Gemma. 'This building used to be a pickle factory and the onion vinegar permeated the bricks.' She handed Luke's book to the woman behind the reception desk — a serious lady wearing a badge on her bosom proclaiming her to be 'Rita. Assistant Librarian'. The computer calculated the fine and Rita held out her hand.

'Velma, have you got any cash?' asked Gemma.

Velma searched her pockets. 'I've got a bit, I think.'

There was a brief hiatus while the two officers laid their change out on the desk and decided who should pay. They eventually stumped up half each.

'Are you friends of Luke?' asked Rita. 'Only we haven't seen him in here for a while. He used to come most days to do some research on our computers. I hope he isn't ill.'

'I'm afraid Mr Burton has passed away,' explained Velma delicately.

'Oh dear,' said Rita. 'But he was so young. Was it an accident?'

Velma decided it was neither appropriate nor necessary to explain the circumstances of Luke's death. Rita obviously hadn't read the graphic account in the *Richington*

Echo, although Velma could see several copies available in the newspaper section of the library. 'Do you know what Mr Burton was researching on the PCs?'

'No, I'm afraid I don't.' Rita chewed her lip. 'Only that it kept him very busy. Mack might know. That's him over there, having his lunch.' She indicated an old man in a shabby raincoat, sitting at one of the magazine tables. He was eating fish and chips off a copy of *Breastfeeding Weekly*. 'He and Luke chatted quite a bit. Why don't you ask him?'

They went across and held out their warrant cards. 'It's Mack, isn't it? May we have a word, please?'

'Oh. You're coppers. Pity. And there was me thinking I was being propositioned. Mind you, we don't get many ladies of the night in here on a wet Wednesday afternoon. What can I do for you, officers?'

'We understand you were a friend of Luke Burton,' began Gemma.

Mack frowned. 'Yes, I knew the lad. Bad business, that. I read about it in the *Echo*. Who'd do a terrible thing like that to a decent, harmless young man, just because he sang in a choir? And now they say an elderly lady has been murdered, too, for the same reason. It defies belief.'

'We were hoping you'd be able to tell us something else about Luke,' said Velma. She ignored this theory as she was not, by any means, signed up to it. 'Something that might help us find his killer.'

'I know he loved his job in the garden centre and singing with Ellie, his girlfriend. He was very fond of her. Reckoned he was going to marry her when they were older. Won't happen now though, will it?'

'Do you know what he was researching on the computers?' Gemma asked.

'Not really. I don't understand all that modern technology malarkey, but I picked up that it was very important to Luke. After each session, he printed out a pile of stuff on the library printer, but he didn't show me. Then the last time he was in, he told me he'd found something amazing. He was really happy. He said he didn't need to look any more, shook my hand and wished me good luck. I never saw him again.'

'And you've no idea what it was that he'd found?' Velma asked.

'None. Sorry, love. I'd help if I could.'

'Well, thanks anyway.' They turned to leave, then Velma remembered something. 'Did he ever show you an old photograph?'

'You mean the one of a young lassie, holding a bairn? Yes, he always carried it in the pocket of his jacket. He never told me who it was, though.'

CHAPTER TEN

Felicity Thomas was posting her final entry before she closed down the Richington Community Choir blog for good.

It is with great regret that due to the sad loss of three key members, it has become impossible for the Richington Community Choir to continue and, as such, it has been disbanded with immediate effect. The remaining choir members would like to thank their loyal fans for their support and sponsorship over the years, and it is hoped that they may continue to provide choral entertainment at some time in the future. All existing fixtures are hereby cancelled.

And that was that. In a few sentences, the choir, which had been her life and a millstone around her neck for longer than she cared to remember, was summarily terminated. Not that there were many members left anyway.

The murders of the choir members had exerted a profound and devastating impact on the future of the Kings Richington choir. As the community grappled with the horror and uncertainty, the choir members had begun to resign one by one. The once vibrant and harmonious group was now overshadowed by fear and mistrust, making it difficult for anyone to continue participating.

The resignation of choir members was driven by several factors. Firstly, the palpable fear that the murderer could be someone within their own ranks made it impossible for members to feel safe. The thought of rehearsing in the same spaces where their friends had previously stood then been brutally murdered was too much to bear. Secondly, the intense scrutiny and gossip surrounding each member's past and personal life created an environment of suspicion and discomfort. The choir, which had once been a source of joy and community, was now a place of anxiety and dread.

As more members resigned, the choir's ability to function was severely compromised. The loss of key voices and the emotional toll on the remaining members made it difficult to maintain the quality of their performances. Bryn, the choir director, had tried to keep the group together but faced an insurmountable challenge. The sense of unity and camaraderie that had defined the choir was shattered, and the prospect of rebuilding seemed increasingly unlikely.

The community's response to the resignations was mixed. Some understood the members' decisions and sympathized with their plight, while others lamented the loss of a cherished tradition. The church of St Boniface, which had relied on the choir to uplift spirits and bring people together, now faced the reality that the choir might cease to exist. The music that had once filled the church with hope and joy was replaced by silence and sorrow.

In the end, the murders not only took the lives of beloved choir members but also dismantled the very fabric of the choir itself. The future of Kings Richington's choir looked bleak, with the possibility of revival seeming distant. The community was left to mourn not only the loss of their friends but also the loss of a cherished part of their cultural and spiritual life.

Felicity had had emails and phone calls from most members saying they no longer wished to be included in any future engagements and therefore would not be attending practice nights. She could hardly blame them. Who in their right mind would want to be part of any ensemble where the members were being swatted like flies? Well, she for one wouldn't miss it. She had exciting plans for the future which didn't include skivvying for Bryn and making the eternal rock buns. She assumed that as she had never been a member of the choir, she wouldn't be a future target. She heard Bryn's key in the door and looked at the clock. Why was he home at this time of day?

'Bryn? Is that you? Why aren't you at work?'

He appeared in the doorway, dishevelled and, if she wasn't much mistaken, rather the worse for drink.

He threw his jacket on the floor, sank down onto the sofa and put his boots up on the coffee table. 'I've resigned. Packed it in. Walked out.'

'What? Why?'

'Because driving a forklift isn't an appropriate occupation for someone with my outstanding talents and I told them so.' In reality, he'd had to suffer the humiliation of confessing to the fraudulent declaration he'd made on his job application. He'd had no choice because he knew that officious detective, Dawes, and his fat, scruffy sergeant would check up on him. The company had sacked him on the spot and told him to think himself lucky they hadn't reported him to the police for fraud. That Peregrine Lloyd-Snotty-Robinson who walked about as if he had a nasty smell under his nose had passed him as he was leaving and completely blanked him. He'd been right to get out. He was much too good for labouring in a warehouse. Why should he, when Felicity had all that money?

Felicity was shocked. 'But you don't know how to do anything else and you were lucky to get that job with your police record. They'd have sacked you if they'd found out you'd been in prison for violence. What are you going to do for money?'

'You've got plenty. I'll spend yours.' He laughed nastily. 'Let's face it, you're not going to need it, are you? It's not as if you wear make-up or buy expensive sexy underwear. You go about like a dull, dreary drudge, and we don't go out anywhere apart from choir fixtures.'

'Well, there aren't going to be any more of those,' she sneered. 'Your precious loyal singers have all packed it in, too.'

'Good. I'm bored with it anyway. I'm planning a trip to Wales to an Eisteddfod. I'm going to offer my services. They'll jump at the chance of hiring a first-class musician like me.' He went across to the drinks cabinet and poured himself a large brandy. 'I may buy myself a new car. Mine is starting to stutter at high speeds.'

'Not with my money you won't,' she shrieked.

He grabbed her by the shoulders and pushed his face into hers; his beard raked her cheek and his breath stank of stale alcohol. 'Oh, and how are you going to stop me? You forget, when you were young and even more stupid than you are now, you gave me full access to all your cash and it needs both of us to revoke it.' He let her go and strolled about the room, hands in his pockets, kicking at the furniture. 'I'll probably sell this big, ugly mausoleum of a house when your money runs out.'

'Over my dead body,' she fumed.

He laughed. 'If necessary. The police would simply think you were another victim of The Choir Killer.'

'And that's exactly what they'd think if I were to kill you!' she exploded.

He laughed again, a drunken mocking laugh. 'You kill me? And how would you do that? You're not capable.'

She challenged him. 'Everyone's capable of one murder, Bryn. It just needs sufficient provocation. And incidentally, where did you really go the night Charlie Snell was murdered and you lied to the police about being at home?'

'If you must know, I'd arranged to meet him in Richington Forest. The bastard was trying to blackmail me. He'd been having it off with one of the secretaries who worked in the probation office and he found out I'd done time. He was threatening to make it public, so I agreed to meet him and hand over the money, but I was actually going to give him a good thrashing. I lost my way in the dark, then when I finally found the clearing where we'd agreed to meet, he was lying there, already dead. I couldn't believe my luck. What about you?' he countered. 'You lied to the police, too. You went out again after I'd left. I saw your wet coat. Where did you go in the pouring rain?'

She hesitated, then said, 'I went for a walk. Even the rain's preferable to being in the house with you.'

'Well, you're free to bugger off anytime you like, cariad. I'll be glad to see the back of you.'

This time, he'd gone too far. She left the room before she lost control and did something violent. It wasn't the right time, but he'd soon find out what she was capable of. She pressed a speed dial number on her phone.

* * *

The incident room was buzzing with activity and the whiteboard was crammed with images and scribbled names and more connecting arrows.

At the end of each shift, Aled updated the whiteboard to ensure that the team had a clear understanding of the current status of the investigation. This continuity was crucial for maintaining momentum and ensuring a seamless transition between shifts. His methods were thorough. When an eyewitness reported seeing a suspicious vehicle near Richington Forest, the lead was added to the high-priority section with details about the vehicle and the witness. It had turned out to be a courting couple. Any new theory discussed during a briefing was updated to the whiteboard to reflect it and any related leads. Where a potential suspect had been investigated and found to be irrelevant, Aled marked the lead as closed. Where surveillance footage revealed a new suspect, a profile was created and any connections to crime scenes were mapped out. Different colours indicated the priority and status of leads, red for high priority, yellow for medium, green for low, and blue for closed.

It had developed into a spider's web with Charlie Snell, the first corpse, at the centre. Arrows led outwards to a grim picture of Luke, lying in a pool of his own blood. The image the SOCO had taken of Violet with a knitting needle in her ear Aled had considered too sad and gruesome, so he had replaced it with a choir publicity photo. After that, there were scribbled messages describing everything relevant that the background checks had uncovered and speculative comments on motives and alibis.

'Sir,' Aled called out, 'we have an update from Dr Hardacre on the lab reports.' He read out the information in the email so everyone in the room could hear. 'The fingerprints on the passports that were taken from Snell's shed belonged to Charlie, Doreen Snell, Bradley Snell and numerous others, presumably the original owners. Uniform is locating them and pulling them in. Will they be charged?'

'Too right, they will,' confirmed Bugsy. 'Passports, even expired ones, are the property of the government. They have to be sent to the Passport Office to be disposed of properly. It's a crime to sell one for nefarious purposes.'

'At least we've managed to keep this consignment out of the hands of Snell's contacts,' said Jack. 'What else have you got, Aled?'

'The fingerprints on the knitting needle that killed Mrs Dibble were difficult to isolate, but the lab says they're her own and Dr Amory's from when she touched it in an attempt to pull it out.'

There were sounds of disgust around the room and gulps of revulsion.

'You have to hand it to Dr Amory,' commented Gemma. 'She has a strong stomach.'

'She'll need it if she's planning on being the next mayor,' said Bugsy. 'All those civic and ceremonial functions, shaking sweaty hands while kids wipe their sticky fingers on your robes and pull your chain. I wonder what her husband thinks of it.'

'I doubt whether Julian Amory cares one way or the other,' remarked Clive. 'He'll be too occupied trying to prevent his business from going under. His finances are in a hell of a state and some aspects of it look decidedly dodgy.'

'Are we talking fraud, here?' asked Jack.

'Almost certainly, sir. We may need to notify the Serious Fraud Office and Companies House about some of it. It looks like his house is about to be repossessed, and short of a miracle, he'll be declared bankrupt.'

'That will put the kibosh on Elizabeth Amory's lofty ambitions,' observed Gemma. 'I wonder what she's doing about it.'

'If I'm any judge,' offered Bugsy, 'she won't even notice until the shit hits the fan and the bailiffs are taking her furniture away. She's too wrapped up in all her good works. It won't half come as a shock when she finds out.'

'Happily, fraud and bankruptcy are the responsibilities of departments other than ours. Was there anything else Dr Hardacre wanted to tell MIT?' asked Jack.

'Yes, sir,' replied Aled. 'She says she's sure you'll have picked up on it already, but it's interesting to note that in each of the three murders, the killer has used a weapon convenient to his or her location at the time — a tree branch in the forest, pruning shears in the garden centre and now a needle from the victim's knitting. She's not sure what to make of it but points out that you're the detective, so it's down to you to work it out.'

'Had we picked up on that, sir?' asked Chippy.

'Er . . . yes, I'm sure we had — subliminally, anyway. Any conclusions, folks?'

'I suppose the obvious one is that in each case, the perpetrator didn't decide to kill until moments before they did it. Something happened in those last few seconds to trigger it.' Velma was drawing on her forensic psychological experience with real case studies. 'So it's unlikely to have been a deep-seated dislike of the choir *per se* — only specific members of it and possibly for completely different reasons.'

'If that's right,' said Chippy, 'how do we know who's going to be next?'

'We don't,' said Jack, 'which means we have to catch this killer or killers before he or she can strike again. Gemma, Velma, anything to report from Luke Burton's flat?'

'Not much, sir,' said Gemma. 'He didn't own a laptop, but he did a considerable amount of research on the computers in the library and printed off a lot of stuff, though we didn't find any of it in his flat.'

'We found the last library book that he borrowed,' added Velma. 'It was all about genetics. It seems that was the subject he was studying. We made enquiries about how he seemed the last time he went there and the consensus was that he was in good spirits, having found what he was looking for.'

'Not much to help with why he was suddenly stabbed in the garden centre then. Aled, Chippy, how did you get on with Mrs Dibble's neighbours? Did they see or hear anything suspicious on the day she was murdered?'

'Nope, nothing, sir,' Chippy answered.

'Diddly squat,' confirmed Aled.

'I spoke to an elderly gentleman who reckoned the council wants to evict all the residents of Sunny Homes so they can let the bungalows as holiday cottages to tourists at a much higher rent,' reported Chippy. 'But he had a serious chip on his shoulder and didn't have anything good to say about anybody. He kept going on about officials lining their own pockets and brown envelopes changing hands, so I didn't take it seriously.'

'Wouldn't you think,' observed Bugsy, 'that elderly people living in a close-knit community with time on their hands and the natural curiosity that comes with age would have noticed *something*? Instead of which, our murderer waltzes in off the street, skewers an old lady with her own knitting needle, then just waltzes out again.'

'We're missing something, Sarge.' Aled was baffled. 'I don't know what, but I reckon it's staring us right in the face. What I can't get out of my head is that dear old Violet was knitting me a sweater with that needle.'

'OK, folks,' said Jack. 'Let's call it a day. The weekend beckons. We'll give it another go on Monday.'

Everyone shambled out, discussing their plans for the weekend. Aled always worked out in the gym on Friday nights, Velma was going to a Kafka play with friends, and Gemma intended to pick up a takeaway on the way home and spend the evening in front of the TV in her pyjamas. Clive was working on creating a new app using AI and Bugsy had promised to take Iris out for a meal. Jack was destined for a night in on his own as both Corrie and Carlene were catering an important engagement party and wouldn't be home until late. Everyone had plans except Chippy. He was keen to make his way in the police service and decided he would spend the next hour or two looking through PACE, the Act of Parliament that gave police officers the powers to combat crime, and he was particularly keen to learn the codes of practice that had to be observed when exercising those powers. He was deep in concentration when Aled's phone rang. He went across and answered it. 'Hello, Metropolitan Police. How can I help?'

'Hello. This is Jim Scuttle, landlord of the Richington Arms. Can I speak to Detective Constable Williams, please? It's urgent.'

'I'm sorry, DC Williams has left for the weekend. This is DC Chippendale. Can I help at all?'

Jim hesitated. 'Could you perhaps get a message to Aled? I promised I'd let him know when certain individuals came into my pub. Well, they're here now. Three of them this time, and I overheard them talking about setting up another deal — but not in here. Aled will know what I mean.'

'OK, Mr Scuttle. I'll pass on the message. Do you know where this deal is taking place?'

'Yes. They're going to the Golden Goat pub in Richington Malworthy. Tell him to watch his back. It's bandit country.'

CHAPTER ELEVEN

Chippy knew from the team meetings that Charlie Snell had been heavily involved in the passport scam and Inspector Dawes believed it could have been instrumental in his murder. He also knew that fake passports carried a national threat and were taken very seriously by National Crime officers. There was no way he was going to wait until Monday to report this new deal that Jim had mentioned. This was Aled's lead and he'd want to know about it, particularly as it could be closely linked to an MIT murder investigation. He phoned his mobile and listened to the rings until the inevitable redirection to voicemail.

He left a message. 'Aled, mate, this is Chippy. I'm still at the station. There's been a call on your work phone from your contact in the Richington Arms.' He was careful not to mention the name — he'd learned that much since he'd joined the MIT. Informants remained anonymous for fear of reprisals. 'He says the men you're interested in are setting up a new deal and they're relocating to the Golden Goat pub in Richington Malworthy. I'm on my way there now. Join me as soon as you get this message. I'll keep an eye on them until you get here.'

He hurried down to the police car pool then changed his mind. He'd be faster if he went on his motorbike. In addition, his black leathers and a full-face crash helmet would make him less recognizable. He revved up his Suzuki and shot off down the bypass.

* * *

Corrie and Carlene had spent most of the day in the Coriander's Cuisine kitchens preparing the food for the engagement party that evening. The clients had told Corrie to spare no expense. The party was for their much-loved only daughter who was getting engaged to an international financier.

'If the Cuisine makes a really good impression,' said Corrie, 'we might get the contract for the wedding.' With this in mind, she had sourced only the best ingredients from her most reliable producers.

'This is a first-class banquet,' observed Carlene, studying the menu. 'They won't find better this side of London's West End. We just need to get it safely to the venue.' They loaded everything into one of the larger Coriander's Cuisine vans, together with the necessary pans and utensils for preparing the hot food.

'We haven't seen the venue yet,' observed Corrie, 'so I hope the cooking facilities will be up to scratch. I've learned from experience not to assume the equipment on site will be adequate.'

'You'll cope, Mrs D. You always do.'

'Not always. When I first started out as a professional caterer, I was hired to cook a meal for a retired major general. I don't think he'd cooked anything for himself in his life. He probably ate all his meals in the officers' mess. He had an old gas stove in a tiny kitchen the size of a garden shed which he shared with the regimental mascot and a budgie in a cage. I was worried about the safety implications, so I turned off the gas at the mains while I went for a pee, but I left the oven on. When I turned the gas back on again to light one of the rings, there was a massive explosion. The oven door blew open and a huge fireball shot out. It missed the regimental bulldog by inches and all the feathers fell out of the budgie. It took a month for my eyebrows to grow back. It was a lesson I've never forgotten, so now, I go prepared for all eventualities, however primitive.'

'That's one for your memoirs, Mrs D,' giggled Carlene.

When they reached the elegant porticoed house on the genteel side of Richington Malworthy, it was obvious that here, they would find a kitchen with every conceivable convenience.

'Wow!' Carlene looked around at the gleaming quartz worktops and the two big multi-functional double cookers. 'This is mega. Where do you want me to start?'

'You prepare the lobster and prawn canapés and I'll pan-sear the salmon. I've seen the buffet table and it's huge, so we need to make it look spectacular.'

As it turned out, the entire evening was spectacular. Everyone was dressed in brightly coloured party outfits and the happily engaged couple were thrilled with it all, not least the food. So much so that the clients insisted Corrie and Carlene join in dancing with the guests. The music was lively and infectious, and as Carlene said, it was impossible not to want to get up and leap about with everyone else. It was later than usual by the time they finally finished packing all the empty dishes and utensils back into the van and headed for home.

Corrie started the engine. 'Jack said we were to drive straight home without stopping. Apparently, Richington Malworthy isn't a safe place to be at any time, let alone late at night, and the chances of finding a copper if you need one are zero.'

* * *

The Golden Goat was what Chippy reckoned his father meant when he described a pub as 'spit and sawdust'. He parked the bike round the back, took off his crash helmet and pushed open the door. Inside, his nostrils were assailed by the combined stink of stale beer, 'funny' tobacco and sweat. His boots stuck to the floor as he strolled casually towards the grubby wood-panelled bar, which was streaked with a dark red stain that he thought was probably blood. The wonky sign directing customers to the toilets was totally unnecessary, he decided. All you had to do was follow your nose. He wondered how long it had been since they were cleaned. The bloke serving behind the bar had a long scar down one cheek and half his right ear was missing as if it had been bitten or cut off in a fight. He wasn't very talkative, acknowledging customers only with a nod and a grunt. Chippy ordered tonic water and leaned casually against the bar, trying to check out the customers without appearing too interested. He wondered how much longer it would be before Aled arrived because he was feeling far from confident on his own.

An hour later, Aled still hadn't turned up, and as far as he could make out, neither had the three individuals he'd come to observe. Just as he was starting to feel he was wasting his time, an argument broke out over by the pool table. Three swarthy-looking men were having some kind of altercation. Chippy didn't know what they were saying as he didn't recognize the language, but he could tell that one of them was accusing the other two of something. He picked up his glass and sauntered over to a seat close by, hoping he'd be able to pick up some of what the argument was about.

His phone rang. He pulled it out of his pocket and looked at the screen. It was Aled. Relieved, he answered it. 'Aled, you got my message.'

'Chippy, what the hell are you doing? Please tell me you haven't gone to Richington Malworthy on your own.' Aled feared the worst.

'Yes. I'm in the Golden Goat. I think I've found what you're looking for, but I haven't seen any passports change hands yet, although I'm pretty sure something illegal's going on.'

'Have you called for uniform backup?' Aled was talking on his hands-free police radio whilst driving as fast as safety would allow. He'd only just picked up the message, having been working out longer at the gym than he did most Friday nights after work. Then he'd struck up a conversation with a fit young lady in the juice bar and lost track of time.

'No, I haven't,' confessed Chippy. 'Should I have phoned Sergeant Parsloe at the station?' Instantly, Chippy realized it was a bad mistake. Although he hadn't been able to understand their language, the three men had clearly understood him. They stopped arguing and lumbered across, surrounding him. Chippy shoved his mobile in his pocket with Aled still shouting at him on the other end.

'What you want, copper?' asked one of them — a big, bull-necked man almost twice the size of Chippy and covered in tattoos.

'You want trouble?' the second one asked menacingly.

'No . . . er . . .' Chippy sensed this wasn't going to end well and hoped Aled could still hear from inside his jacket pocket.

'You want trouble, we give you trouble. We don't want coppers in here. You come outside.'

They gave him no choice. They lifted him off his seat and strong-armed him through the door. Nobody, including the barman, made any attempt to help him. The few remaining customers carried on drinking, smoking and mindlessly gawping at the football match on the big screen as if violence was a daily occurrence. Given the Richington Malworthy reputation, it probably was. Once outside, the men dragged Chippy down an alleyway alongside the pub.

'Why you come here, copper?' The big one pulled Chippy's wallet and warrant card from his pocket and squinted at it. 'What you know?'

Chippy bluffed, not very successfully. 'I . . . er . . . I don't know anything. I was just having a quiet drink. If you don't let me go, I may have to arrest you for threatening behaviour.'

Laughing, the big one landed the first punch, a crunching blow to the stomach with a massive fist. Chippy sank to his knees, coughing and retching.

'Chippy, what's happening?' Aled's desperate voice came from the phone in Chippy's pocket. 'Are you all right? Speak to me.'

The second thug grabbed the phone, threw it on the ground and stamped on it. After that, the blows came thick and fast. Chippy lost consciousness, but they continued to punch and kick him with heavy fists and boots.

* * *

Corrie and Carlene agreed it had been a great evening, both socially and financially. The clients had added a sizeable gratuity to the fee as they had been so pleased with the spread and booked Coriander's Cuisine to cater the wedding meal as well, putting down a hefty deposit.

Corrie drove purposefully down the dirty, neglected main road through Richington Malworthy, glad to be leaving 'bandit country' behind. Half the street lights had been smashed and gang graffiti adorned virtually every wall and shop front. She sang along to Abba on the car radio to keep up her spirits. 'Dancing queen, feel the beat from the tangerine.'

'What?' laughed Carlene. 'That isn't right, Mrs D. It's a beat from a tambourine. Not a tangerine.'

'Is it? I didn't know that. I thought it was tangerine.'

'That's because your mind's always on food . . .' She broke off suddenly. 'Stop, Mrs D! Back up! There's something going on down that alley next to the pub.'

'What sort of something?' Corrie pulled over cautiously, keeping the engine running.

'Three blokes are beating the shit out of someone. He needs help.' She opened the passenger door and started to scramble out.

'No! Carlene . . . No!' Corrie grabbed her arm. 'I'll call the police and an ambulance.' She was already pushing the emergency button on her phone. 'You mustn't interfere. Jack said it's a dangerous area. Wait for the police.'

'There isn't time,' Carlene shouted. 'The poor guy will be dead by the time they get here. He isn't moving and I can see a lot of blood.' She leaned over, grabbed a cast iron frying pan from the back of the van and leapt out. Running towards the alley, she yelled, 'Leave him alone, you bastards!'

The biggest of the three with the bald head and tattoos saw her coming and lumbered towards her, grinning. As he got close, he drew back his fist to punch her in the face, but before he could make contact, Carlene whacked him around the head with the iron skillet. He yelped and staggered in circles like a concussed boxer.

Corrie, running hotfoot behind Carlene, had turned up the volume on her phone to maximum and was playing the police siren ringtone that Jack used for work calls. Alarmed, the other two thugs exchanged startled glances. Believing the police were nearby, they grabbed their dazed colleague, bundled him into a yellow Ford Cortina and, with wheels spinning on the tarmac, they made off down the road.

Corrie and Carlene saw them go and went to help Chippy. They bent over his broken and bleeding body. 'Dear God, Mrs D, they've made a right mess of this young bloke.'

Corrie felt for a pulse. 'He's still breathing, but he's badly injured.' She frowned. 'He looks vaguely familiar. I think I may have seen him at the station with Jack.'

'Do you mean he's a copper?' asked Carlene.

'Yes, one of the newer detectives.'

Carlene put her mouth close to his ear. 'Can you hear me? What's your name?'

Chippy rallied briefly and muttered something.

'What did he say?' Corrie asked.

'It sounded like "chip",' replied Carlene.

'He's in no condition to eat chips,' declared Corrie. 'What on earth was he doing in a place like this in the first place? They don't even serve chips. I'm sure Jack wouldn't have sent him — not on his own, anyway.'

'I guess we'll find out once he can talk again. I think his jaw's broken and he's lost a few teeth. There's such a lot of blood it's hard to tell.' Carlene suddenly spotted a yellow Ford Cortina in the distance, speeding down the road towards them. 'Quick, Mrs D, they're coming back. I think they've realized the siren was a bluff. We have to get out of here and fast.'

'What about him?' Corrie indicated Chippy, who had passed out again. 'We can't leave him here. Should we take him into the pub until the police and ambulance get here?'

'Definitely not! Remember what the locals at the party said about the Golden Goat? It's a no-go area unless you're a villain and to stay well away. We'll put him in the back of the van. You take his legs.'

'What if they're broken?' fretted Corrie.

'He's still got a better chance than if we leave him behind.'

Between them, they bundled Chippy into the back of the van amongst the pots and pans then jumped in the front, gunned the engine and raced away.

'Floor it, Mrs D!' shouted Carlene. 'They're gaining on us!'

Corrie had never driven a getaway van before, especially not a bright green one with Coriander's Cuisine food decals on the side. By the time she reached the dual carriageway, she was clocking eighty and convinced she could feel her hair turning grey.

* * *

When his phone rang, Jack hoped for a moment that it might be Corrie, telling him she was on her way home. Except it wasn't the 'Food, Glorious Food' ringtone; it was the police siren.

'Sir, it's DC Williams. I'm sorry to ring you on a Friday night, but we have an emergency.'

Jack could tell from Aled's anxious voice that it wasn't trivial and that he was speaking on his car radio, so he was on the move. He got straight to the point. 'What's happened?'

'It's Chippy, sir — DC Chippendale. He's in danger and he's on his own.' Aled explained the situation and how there had been foreign voices shouting and the sound of punches being landed before Chippy's phone had suddenly shut down. 'It's my fault, sir. He was following one of my leads and I should have told him not to go there without backup.'

'Where is "there"?' demanded Jack, already grabbing his coat and car keys.

'The Golden Goat pub in Richington Malworthy, sir.'

Jack's heart missed a beat. Richington Malworthy was where Corrie and Carlene had gone — he'd warned her about taking a catering job in bandit country. He prayed the banquet wasn't anywhere near the Golden Goat. 'I'm on my way. I'll summon up Sergeant Parsloe's cavalry and Sergeant Malone's bulk.' Soon, he was speeding down the bypass, blues and twos activated and with police cars and Bugsy in hot pursuit. Although it wasn't police policy to use the car radio as a phone, he considered this was an emergency with lives in danger. He called Corrie, whose jaws were clamped together in terrified concentration as she saw the yellow Cortina coming ever closer in her wing mirror.

Carlene grabbed the phone. 'Help, Inspector Jack! We're being chased by three thugs in a yellow Cortina and we've got one of your detectives in the back of the van. He's been badly hurt.'

'Where are you?' Jack could feel a cold sensation in the pit of his stomach. Somehow, Corrie and Carlene, the two people he loved most in the world, had got mixed up with men strongly suspected of killing Charlie Snell and who wouldn't hesitate to kill again if cornered. Added to that, it seemed they had DC Chippendale lying injured in the back of the van.

'We're on the dual carriageway out of Richington Malworthy and we're going bloody fast!' Carlene gasped.

Jack, Aled and Bugsy in separate cars were on the dual carriageway going *into* Richington Malworthy in convoy and were also travelling at top speed. Jack pressed the control button next to the steering wheel so the police cars could hear him. 'This is Detective Inspector Dawes. Look out for a green transit van travelling south on the opposite side of the carriageway, being pursued by a yellow Ford Cortina travelling at high speed. The Cortina is being driven by suspects believed to have committed a murder and a serious assault on a police officer. Stop and detain.'

'There they are, sir!' shouted Aled. 'I can see Mrs Dawes' green van. It just shot past in the opposite direction. Bloody hell, she's shifting!'

Bugsy's voice came through on the radio. 'There's a roundabout coming up, guv. We need to make a U-turn.'

The whole convoy screeched around the roundabout almost on two wheels then back up the southbound carriageway. By then, the Cortina was right on the tail of Corrie's van, but behind them, the thugs' exit was now effectively blocked by the police cars, their lights blazing and sirens blaring. Panicking, the Cortina driver lost control and crashed into the central barrier. The doors burst open and the occupants ran for it. There was a lot of shouting and fighting before they were quickly rounded up by Norman's uniformed officers, handcuffed and shoved in the back of police cars, struggling and protesting their innocence.

Moments later, ambulance paramedics were carefully extracting Chippy from the back of the van, putting up a drip, giving him oxygen and stabilizing his broken bones prior to transferring him to the Richington Infirmary.

Jack threaded his way through the melee of police cars until he found Corrie and Carlene sitting on the tailgate of the green van with ambulance blankets around their shoulders. Wordlessly, he hugged them both for some moments, then he spoke. 'Don't you ever do that to me again.'

* * *

Back in the safety of her kitchen, Corrie was gradually recovering from her venture into the world of getaway cars and vicious criminals. At least her teeth had stopped chattering. She was sipping cocoa with a shot of something strong that Jack had put in it. It wasn't the first time that she and Carlene had accidentally got embroiled in danger, but this time, it had been a close call. She was expecting a telling-off.

'Before you say it, Jack, Carlene and I weren't interfering in police business.'

'No, we weren't,' confirmed Carlene. 'Well, not really — and we had the best of intentions. And before you say it, yes, I know that the road to hell is paved with them.'

Corrie continued. 'We'd just completed a very successful booking and were on our way home, minding our own business, when Carlene spotted your constable being beaten to within an inch of his life. We could have just driven past and left him, but we didn't. How is he, by the way?'

'Amongst other things, DC Chippendale has several broken bones, a ruptured spleen and liver damage, but the doctors say he's young and strong and he'll recover.' Jack was not to be diverted from his lecture. 'To be fair, you probably saved his life, but it was still a very dangerous thing for two women to attempt on their own.'

'Two women and a frying pan,' muttered Carlene under her breath.

CHAPTER TWELVE

Jack had been summoned upstairs to a meeting with Commander Sir Barnaby, Chief Superintendent Garwood and two senior officers from the National Crime Agency. In DCS Garwood's plush office, the men were sitting around the table Garwood used for meetings. His personal assistant had brought tea and biscuits and withdrawn discreetly.

Garwood was convinced that the object of the meeting was to reprimand Dawes officially for not realizing sooner that passport crimes had been taking place on his watch. He decided it wouldn't do his own career any harm if he got in first with the dressing-down. He needed to demonstrate he was in total control of his division and that he demanded and received their total respect. He began, 'Detective Inspector Dawes, I have been meaning to speak to you about the way you handled the business with the illegal passports.'

'Absolutely,' interrupted the Commander. 'Excellent work, Jack. If your team hadn't been on the ball, the NCA might never have caught the criminals and traced the organization that has been financing them from abroad. I hope your young DC is going to be all right.'

'Yes, Commander,' confirmed Jack. 'He's getting there, thank you, sir. I'll pass on your comments to the team.'

'Er . . . yes . . . Jack. Well done. That's what I was just about to say.' Garwood winced at how close he had come to putting his foot in it. Bloody Dawes had come up smelling of roses — again! He felt in his pocket for an indigestion tablet, then tried to recover his grip on the proceedings. 'Do we think those men were responsible for the murder of Charlie Snell?'

'They're saying not,' replied the NCA officer. 'My agents have been questioning them individually for some hours with a solicitor and interpreters present to make certain they can't accuse us of any funny business. Whilst they admit conspiring with him regarding the fake passports, they firmly deny any involvement in his death.'

'Do you believe them, sir?' asked Jack.

'Yes, if only because they had nothing to gain from it. They say he was one of their best suppliers, using the butcher's shop as a front — a kind of bureau de change for illegal passports. Once they realized their nice little earner was over, they were quite obliging and gave us good leads on their other contacts. Of course they're looking at long sentences, not least because of the attack on your detective constable. One thing seemed a little strange. The ringleader said he would cooperate as long we kept "mad woman with cooking pan" away from him. Do you know who he means?'

'I think I do,' said Jack, smiling to himself. 'Tell him she is safely under control.'

* * *

Back down in the incident room, the atmosphere was sombre. One of their own had been badly hurt in the line of duty and what was going through everyone's head was that it could just as easily have been any one of them.

Aled was particularly affected. 'How is Chippy, Sarge? He is going to make it, isn't he?'

'Yes, son,' Bugsy reassured him. 'The doctors say he'll recover, but it may take a while and he'll have to take it easy in the meantime.'

Clearly agitated, Aled pushed back his chair, stood up and began to pace around the room. 'It was my fault, wasn't it? First Mrs Dibble and now Chippy.' He ran distraught fingers through his hair. 'Anyone working with me is doomed. I'm a jinx — a curse.'

'Oh, get over yourself!' scolded Gemma. 'Chippy was showing initiative, however misguided, and nobody could possibly have foreseen how it would turn out.'

'Having a meltdown isn't going to help, son.' Bugsy remembered having been where Aled was now — feeling personally responsible for another officer's injuries. He recalled that it hadn't been so long ago that a young constable, barely a month in the job and under his supervision, had taken two bullets in the chest because, he, Bugsy, couldn't run fast enough to protect him from a killer who was trying to escape. Miraculously, the lad hadn't died, but it had been touch and go for many days and had affected Bugsy enormously. He had stayed by his bedside, day and night, until the lad was out of danger.

'As for Mrs Dibble,' added Velma, 'if my hunch is right, she was killed for an altogether different reason than because she thought she was helping you.'

Suitably chastened, Aled sat down again. 'OK, so what you're saying is it's business as usual, and to pull myself together and get on with it. We need to find out who's targeting the choir before another one's bumped off. Back to the whiteboard, then.' Aled drew arrows linking Charlie Snell, Luke Burton and Violet Dibble. 'We're still looking for a resourceful killer — able to improvise an MO in the heat of the moment. Which is a great way to confuse us. The one common thread we have to go on is the choir. The passport scam was just a distraction.'

'According to Felicity Thomas's latest blog, there isn't a choir to wipe out any longer. It's been disbanded — at least for the time being,' reported Clive.

'Is that going to be enough for our killer?' asked Gemma. 'Having successfully put an end to the choir, does that mean all the other members are out of danger?'

'If that was the killer's motive, then yes, I guess it does,' said Velma.

'You don't sound convinced,' remarked Bugsy.

'That's because I'm not.'

* * *

When Jack heard that Chippy's parents had arrived from New Zealand and were at the hospital, he went straight there to speak to them. He did, after all, have a duty of care and he feared it would seem to them that he hadn't fulfilled it. He remembered Chippy saying that he'd grown up in a happy, loving home with brothers and sisters, which must have been in New Zealand. He wondered what had prompted him to come to the UK and join the police service. When he got to the hospital, he discovered that Chippy had been moved from the Intensive Care Unit to a private room with a dedicated nurse and it was there that Jack met Mr and Mrs Chippendale.

'You must be Detective Inspector Dawes. Oliver speaks about you a lot during our online chats. He thinks very highly of you.' Chippy's father was a distinguished-looking man in his fifties wearing a lightweight suit and crisp white shirt. 'I'm Aubrey Chippendale and this is my wife, Professor Alicia Taylor-Chippendale.' He shook Jack's hand, but Mrs Chippendale hardly spared him a glance, busying herself with smoothing her son's pillows. She wore her hair scraped back into a severe bun and her beige dress and jacket were clearly of the expensive designer variety, but it was clear she had no time for the diktats of fashion.

Jack realized that it was the first time he'd heard Chippy's real name. It suited him. 'Oliver is doing very well, Mr Chippendale. He's a very conscientious member of the team and a fast learner. It was whilst he was following an important lead that he came up against some serious criminals. Obviously, the team is very concerned about him and we want him back on the strength as soon as he's well enough.'

'Well, that isn't going to happen.' Professor Taylor-Chippendale acknowledged Jack's presence at last. 'As soon as the consultants consider him fit to be moved, Oliver is coming home with us to New Zealand.' She turned back to her son, effectively dismissing any further discussion on the subject.

Aubrey Chippendale was conciliatory. 'You see, Inspector, my wife never wanted Ollie to join the police, but it's all he's ever wanted. Even as a little boy, he wanted to be a detective, solving murders in urban England, like the characters on TV. While other boys were reading Superman comics, Oliver was reading Sherlock Holmes.'

'Yes, and look where it got him!' Professor Chippendale snapped. 'He was nearly killed. I'm taking him home and that's the end of it.'

Driving back to the station, Jack understood her feelings, but he knew the team would be sorry to lose Chippy. He had become a lively and imaginative colleague with a quirky take on the job — qualities that would be missed. When the team was disheartened, it was always Chippy who cheered them up and restored their motivation. He would be difficult to replace.

* * *

Elizabeth Amory was extremely irritated. She'd had a very important meeting with the head of Richington Local Authority with regard to her candidacy for local mayor and more hustings were imminent. It had become clear to her that it was going to take significant amounts of money to mount what she would consider a satisfactory campaign. She had put so much effort into her public image already that she wasn't about to cut corners now. Obviously the money wouldn't be a problem, but when she'd phoned the bank manager and asked him to transfer a few thousand into her campaign account to cover initial expenses, he'd behaved very oddly. She and Julian had dined with him and his wife at Julian's club on numerous occasions and she had considered them friends, but now he was being what she could only describe as distant and evasive. She almost suspected he might be keeping something from her. Eventually, he'd told her to go and speak to her husband. It was very tiresome.

On the way home, she'd stopped to pick up a few groceries, but the card reader had rejected her card, which was most inconvenient. She decided the chip must be corrupt and she'd need to get a new one. She tried a different card, but that was rejected, too. Fortunately, she was carrying enough cash to pay for the items. She told the assistant in no uncertain terms that his card reader was faulty and he needed to get it mended.

When she pulled into the drive of the large detached house with the black and white pseudo-Tudor facade, the first thing she noticed was that Julian's Jaguar wasn't there. He hadn't told her he'd be out for supper, which was most remiss of him. She'd noticed he'd been behaving strangely of late and put it down to a mid-life crisis, the male menopause — or some such nonsense that men dream up to excuse their lack of gumption.

She put her key in the lock, pushed open the door with her free hand and reached out to put the groceries on the hall table — except it wasn't there. When she walked through to the living room, it was bare and Julian was sitting on the floor, clutching various documents without looking at them and holding one last glass of single malt that the bailiffs had allowed him to keep. As the man in charge had said, 'We're not complete Philistines, sir.'

Momentarily speechless, she dropped the shopping bag on the floor. Two artichokes and a celeriac bulb fell out. Elizabeth looked around at the empty room and tried to stay calm. What on earth had the idiot done this time? 'Julian, where has all our furniture gone?'

He gazed up at her with a vacant expression. 'The bailiffs took it, my love, and my car. They'll be coming for yours imminently.'

'Don't be silly! What are you talking about?'

'We have massive debts and no money to pay them.' It was a simple explanation of the facts, but she didn't accept it.

'That's rubbish, Julian. What about this house and our savings? We have hundreds of thousands in investments.'

'Not any longer. We're broke.' He drained the last of the whisky.

She decided he must be ill or unhinged. 'Stop it! I don't believe you. Where has it all gone?'

'You squandered most of it on your good works and your quest to become the perfect community member. I made some bad business decisions and I gambled the rest. They'll be coming to take the keys to the house soon and change the locks. I'll be arrested for embezzlement and fraud and I have no credible defence. In the absence of a suitable alternative, I would be spending a sizeable chunk of such years as I have left in HMP Wandsworth, and that really isn't my style. This is the parting of the ways, my love.'

She gulped, having to believe him. The effect that this catastrophe would have on her carefully contrived lifestyle slowly began to dawn on her. 'How am I going to campaign for mayor, never mind Parliament? Julian, you've no idea what lengths I've had to go to, to ensure my reputation stays intact and I remain an eligible candidate for election. What am I supposed to do now? Where am I going to go?'

'Perhaps you could persuade a member of the caring community to take you in until you can find a job. That's what community means, doesn't it?' The doorbell rang. He got up and looked out of the window at the police cars in the drive. 'That's the fuzz coming to arrest me. Don't open the door yet; there's something I have to do first, before they come in.' He kissed her on the cheek. 'Cheerio, dear.'

He left the room but didn't answer the door. The doorbell rang several times more. Then she heard the gunshot.

Elizabeth wasn't taking in what the Serious Fraud Officer was saying. Something about serving a Section 2 notice and allowing him and the police to enter the premises. She stared at them, mindlessly. Sudden stress overload had caused her brain to become detached from her situation, unable to distinguish what was real from what she was imagining. She opened the door wider and stood back, allowing them access. One of the police officers was asking her name, but she couldn't speak. Instead, she pointed towards Julian's study.

* * *

'Did we know Dr Amory's husband had a gun, sir?' asked Aled.

'He didn't have a licence for it,' said Clive, tapping keys. 'I daresay it was inherited from an elderly relative. It was a Webley .38 — standard issue during World War Two.'

'Wherever he got it, it made a nasty mess of his head.' Bugsy was reading the pathology report. 'This report says he sustained "catastrophic injuries consistent with a gunshot wound to the right temporal bone at close range". There doesn't seem to be any doubt that it was suicide. He was the only person in the room and there were only his prints on the gun. The Serious Fraud lads had arrived with the cops to take him away, seconds before he did it. He knew the game was up.'

'If the bailiffs had taken all the furniture away, I wonder where he'd hidden the gun.' Velma always wanted loose ends well-knotted.

'They found soot on it that the lab matched to the open fireplace in his study,' answered Clive. 'He had it hidden up the chimney.'

'Poor Dr Amory,' said Gemma. 'It must have been a terrible shock. I wonder if she even suspected how bad things had become.'

'Do you remember what the Sarge said when I found evidence of Amory's fraud and gambling and that his company was bankrupt?' asked Clive. 'He said he doubted whether Dr Amory paid any attention to the state of their finances and wouldn't notice anything was wrong until the bailiffs arrived.

You had it absolutely right, Sarge. On the same day it happened, she'd phoned the bank manager to ask for five grand to kick off her campaign. He told me she was furious when he told her she couldn't have it. He told her to speak to her husband. I bet she knew nothing until then, just assumed the money would keep coming and she could keep spending it.'

'My ex-wife was like that,' muttered one of the older civilian workers.

'You have to wonder,' mused Jack, 'whether the editor of the *Echo* will try to make a connection between Amory's death and the person he's calling "The Choir Killer". Something along the lines of, *Did the killer murder the contralto's husband by mistake?* Never mind that they've already reported it as a suicide.'

'Surely even the *Echo* wouldn't scrape that particular barrel,' said Aled.

'I wouldn't bet on it. A story's a story — he wouldn't let the truth spoil it. But as far as MIT is concerned, we're still investigating three murders. Suicide is outside our jurisdiction. DC Dinkley, you've been strangely silent recently,' remarked Jack. 'You usually have a hypothesis about everything, but you haven't said much about these choir murders. I sense something obscure brewing in your complex brain that the rest of us mere mortals haven't spotted. Do you want to share it with the team? We need all the help we can get.'

She hesitated. 'It's a long shot, sir, but it's to do with Mrs Dibble's murder. I've been looking at Dr Amory's statement and the pathology report again.'

'And very gruesome reading they make,' commented Bugsy.

'It's more of an anomaly with the timings,' Velma decided.

'You're not going all psychological on us, are you?' asked Aled. 'Only I, for one, will need an interpreter.'

'No, it's fairly straightforward, actually. Dr Amory said in her statement that she had found Mrs Dibble dead at one thirty. She went there in her capacity as chief co-ordinator of FORE — Friends of Richington's Elderly — to take her a vegan cheese and pickle sandwich for Violet's lunch.'

'So where's the timing anomaly?' asked Bugsy, already puzzled.

'In the pathology report, Dr Hardacre put time of death at around noon. She also recorded — and this is the interesting part — that the contents of Mrs Dibble's stomach showed a partly digested cheese sandwich.'

'I see where you're going with this,' said Aled. 'If Dr Amory didn't get there until one thirty and Mrs Dibble died at noon, she couldn't have eaten the cheese sandwich.'

'Exactly,' said Velma. 'That means Dr Amory got there before noon, gave Mrs Dibble the sandwich then while they were chatting, Mrs Dibble must have said or done something that triggered Dr Amory to kill her with the nearest weapon. Knowing that our pathologist would record the correct time of death, she waited an hour and a half before reporting finding Violet's body. She didn't dare leave in case someone else found it. Her DNA and prints were already on the knitting needle, so she had to be the first one on the scene to explain why.'

'That's ghastly!' exclaimed Gemma. 'It means she stuck a knitting needle in that poor old lady's ear then sat there with her dead body until she considered enough time had elapsed that it was safe to tell someone. Why didn't she raise the alarm as soon as she'd killed her?'

'Because that would have made her the prime suspect,' replied Velma. 'She needed significant time between the murder and her alleged arrival on the scene for the killer to have been someone else who had been and gone. Dr Amory's profile is one of an intelligent, educated sociopath with more than a hint of cunning. Even though she didn't go there intending to murder Mrs Dibble, once she'd done it, her mind would have gone immediately into overdrive with self-preservation uppermost.'

'Hang on a minute,' said Bugsy. 'I can see a flaw in your theory — two in fact. First, CCTV would have recorded Dr Amory going in at noon and not half past one, like she claimed, and second, Mrs Dibble could have eaten a cheese sandwich at any time before Dr Amory got there. What do you say to that?'

'Bugsy, there weren't any CCTV cameras outside the bungalows,' interrupted Jack. 'Remember the warden told us the residents demanded they were removed because they thought it was snooping? There was even a petition.'

'OK, but what about CCTV in the street outside? Clive?'

'Yes, Sarge, but the camera is a long way down the road. Even if we found her on it, it wouldn't be enough to implicate her. A decent barrister would claim she was going about her community business in the area, before she went to the Sunny Homes Village.'

'OK, so what about the sandwich? How do we know Mrs Dibble hadn't already eaten one before Dr Amory got there?' Bugsy wasn't about to give up. As far as he was concerned, when you were dealing with murder, any hypothesis had to be tested to destruction.

'Pathology identified it as vegan cheese and pickle, Sarge,' said Velma, delivering her *coup de grâce*.

'And Violet was very definitely not vegan,' added Aled. 'She had no time for what she called 'picky eaters'. She said it was just a fad and very unhealthy. In her day, you ate what was put in front of you and were grateful for it. She wouldn't have kept vegan cheese in her fridge, but she would have eaten the sandwich Dr Amory brought, out of politeness.'

'Well done, Velma,' said Jack. 'Very well thought out. At the very least, it means we need to ask Dr Amory a lot more questions. Let's bring her in.'

'Don't forget her hubby has just topped himself,' warned Bugsy. 'We're members of a modern, sympathetic police service; we don't want to be accused of harassing a bereaved widow.'

'That woman's hard as nails!' exclaimed Gemma. 'As you know, I'm a firm supporter of gender equality and putting an end to sexist exploitation and oppression' — she paused until the exaggerated yawns, sighs and groans died down — 'but Elizabeth Amory represents a version of feminist immorality that does not belong in a civilized society.'

There were murmurs of agreement from the officers grouped around the water cooler.

'She certainly has some serious questions to answer regarding poor Violet,' said Aled, 'and the sooner we bring her in, the better.'

'Do we even know where to find her?' wondered Clive, looking at his screen. 'It says here the house has been repossessed and it's now empty. The lenders are looking for a fast sale at auction. She doesn't seem to have any close relatives, and according to the bank records, she doesn't have access to any cash. Where has she gone?'

CHAPTER THIRTEEN

Elizabeth Amory was sitting on the floor of what used to be her bedroom. Originally, the bailiffs had left items required for basic domestic needs, but these had been cleared out when the bank repossessed the house. Now she had nothing apart from the cash in her handbag and what she had taken with her when they escorted her out. The court bailiff had changed all the locks and cut off the utilities, including the burglar alarms, so she had climbed in through a window in the sun lounge. The catch had been faulty for months and she'd nagged Julian to get someone in to fix it, but he'd never got around to it.

Now, she was sitting on the pale square of carpet where the bed used to be, eating a vegan sandwich that she'd bought from the shop on the corner. It was pretty disgusting, but they'd taken her car, so she couldn't get to M&S. Aware that the couple of hundred pounds in her handbag wouldn't last long, she was forced to assess recent events and how they impacted her carefully planned future. She had intended to burn the printed-out birth records she had snatched from Luke Burton but hadn't found an opportunity before everything blew up in her face. If only the stupid boy hadn't been so stubborn and intent on finding her, none of this would have happened. And when he announced how thrilled he was to have her as his mother, and he intended to proclaim it to the world, declare it on social media, he simply had to be stopped. OK, he hadn't been responsible for her present impecunious circumstances. That was all down to Julian. She should have kept a closer eye on what the idiot was doing. He never did have a grip on what was important in life. How he'd managed to run a company as long as he did was a mystery.

She glanced at the torn photograph of herself at barely sixteen, holding Luke as a baby, and thought she looked dim-witted. That's exactly what she had been, if she was honest. She barely remembered the man who'd got her pregnant. At the time, he had seemed the best prospect to provide her with the life she had mapped out for herself. Of course, he turned out to be married, and after she told him she was pregnant, she didn't see him for dust. She had given up the baby as soon as it was born. That photograph was the only time she had held him, and then only at the insistence of the midwife who claimed she *'would regret it later if she didn't'*, which was rubbish. Even at sixteen, she had known there would be no glowing professional future for a young woman with a child in tow, a child conceived when she was little more than a child herself.

With the support of her parents, the young, ruthless Elizabeth had thrown herself into education and eventually gained a doctorate in theology. It enabled her to put letters after her name, assume a pious disposition and continue with her quest for the perfect life. And the rest, she decided, was consigned to history — because now, there really wasn't any future.

* * *

It was knocking-off time when Bugsy's phone rang. It was Sergeant Parsloe on the desk. 'Norman, my old Woodentop, it's nearly seven o'clock. Haven't you got a home to go to? Or has the fragrant Mrs Parsloe kicked you out at last?'

'Bugsy, I've had a call from a concerned member of the public and I thought you should know straight away.'

'Don't tell me — Chief Superintendent Garwood has been exposing himself in Sainsbury's again.'

'No, it's nothing like that. Be serious, Bugsy. This member of the public lives in the house across the road to Dr Amory.'

'I thought she'd been evicted after the house was repossessed,' said Bugsy. 'We're looking for her in connection with the knitting needle murder.'

'Well, if you get a move on, you might catch her. The caller said she's still in the house. He can see someone moving about and there's a candle burning. I've sent a couple of my PCs to secure the place until you get there.'

'Roger that, Norman. We're on it.' He shouted to Jack, who was just putting on his coat. 'Guv, it's the woman!'

'Irene Adler or Elizabeth Amory?'

'What?' Bugsy was confused. 'Who's Irene Adler?'

'Never mind.' Jack grinned. Unlike Chippy, Bugsy clearly wasn't a Sherlock Holmes fan. 'Where is Dr Amory?'

'Back in the house. Norman's sent two PCs to keep her there.'

'Right. Let's go.'

* * *

PC Jonny Johnson was standing guard by the front porticoed entrance and the other PC had gone round to cover the back. They didn't try to enter, having been told to wait for MIT.

Jack edged the car into the drive and switched off the lights. They climbed out, walked up the drive and looked up at the bedroom window where a candle was still burning. 'Anybody in or out, Jonny?' asked Jack.

'No, sir. Do you want me to force an entry?'

'Let's try the civilized way first.' Jack pressed the bell push.

From the bedroom, Elizabeth heard the familiar chimes of Bach's Toccata and Fugue in D minor. She made a mental note that it was rather less *maestoso* than the composer intended and the batteries needed replacing. Then she remembered that this wasn't her house anymore. She looked out of the window and saw the police cars. They had come for her. She could try to escape through the sun lounge window, but where would she run to? Without money, she'd be persona non grata with all the 'friends' she and Julian had made, and the community wasn't an option. No, she might just as well go down and give herself up. She couldn't be sure how much they knew, but she was sure that the Detective Inspector would have worked most of it out. He was no fool.

She went down and shouted to them through the letterbox. 'I can't let you in. The bailiffs have changed the locks and I don't have a key.'

'You can open it using the thumb turn, Madam,' called PC Johnson.

They could hear her fiddling with it, then the door opened.

'Dr Amory?' asked Jack politely.

'You know I am, Inspector,' she snapped. 'Shall we get this over with?'

They put her in the police car and PC Johnson and his colleague took her off to the station.

'Are you going to question her tonight, guv?' asked Bugsy.

Jack looked at his watch. 'No. I'll caution her and arrest her on suspicion of murder. She can spend a night in one of Norman's cells and talk to her flash and probably very expensive solicitor. We'll speak to her in the morning.'

'The evidence is really only circumstantial at this stage, guv. Do you think we'll get enough to charge her?'

'Yes, I do. Most criminal convictions are based on circumstantial evidence. There just needs to be enough of it to meet recognized standards of proof. In any case, I think she's run out of options and she knows it.'

'Do you reckon she'll apply for bail?' Bugsy wondered.

Jack shook his head. 'The woman's a magistrate. She knows the ropes. If she's done half of what I think she's done, she won't even bother. Added to which, she doesn't have a permanent address now, and that's one of the conditions.'

'Go home, guv. Eat one of those excellent suppers that your missus cooks up. My Iris has made stew and dumplings. I've a feeling we're going to need our strength tomorrow.'

* * *

'So what's new down the nick?' Corrie was spooning lamb bhuna onto Jack's plate.

'Busy Lizzie's behind bars,' announced Jack, helping himself to naan bread.

'What?' squealed Corrie. A whole dish of pakoras skidded across the table and onto the floor.

'We're holding her on suspicion.' Jack tore pieces off the bread and dipped them in his curry.

'On suspicion of what?' Corrie wanted to know. 'Surely you can't arrest someone for being a self-serving, overbearing, arrogant, holier-than-thou pain in the neck, otherwise half the population of Kings Richington would be inside.'

'No, it's more serious than just being irritating,' said Jack. 'She's under arrest for murder.'

'No, not Julian! I can't believe she shot her husband. The *Echo* said it was *a clear case of suicide due to insuperable financial difficulties*.'

'It was. No doubt about it. Pathology proved it.'

'Well, who is Busy Lizzie supposed to have topped, then? She's a Doctor of Theology — someone who studies God and religion. They don't go around murdering people. She doesn't even believe in killing animals for food. Are you sure you've got this right, Jack?'

'Pretty sure. I'm interviewing her in the morning concerning the death of Violet Dibble.'

'Surely not!' Corrie couldn't believe it. 'What possible reason could Busy Lizzie have to kill a harmless old lady like Violet? It doesn't make any sense.'

'Not at the moment it doesn't, but I'm going to ask Velma to sit in; she has a good feel for what makes people like Dr Amory tick and why they commit crimes. It could make all the difference to the outcome.' He pointed to the pakoras on the floor. 'Might I have one of those after you've brushed off the fluff?'

* * *

Sergeant Parsloe intercepted Jack when he arrived at the station next morning. 'Dr Amory has been escorted into Interview Room One, Jack. She's been searched and her possessions are being kept by the custody officer. I asked if she wanted anybody notified that she was here. She said there wasn't anyone who needed to know.'

'OK, Norman. Has she had breakfast?' Jack had missed his on account of sleeping late. He'd had this nightmare where Elizabeth Amory had stuck a knitting needle in his ear and it had gone straight through and come out the other side. He woke up, still wondering what had happened to his brain.

'Yes, we've given her breakfast,' confirmed Norman. 'She asked for scrambled tofu, mushrooms, tomatoes and vegan coffee. I sent one of the lads out to get it from the vegan café down the road.'

'Right.' Jack braced himself. 'We'd better make a start, then.'

'She's very calm, Jack. It's almost as if she thinks she's about to chair one of her meetings instead of answer questions about a murder.'

'Maybe that's her way of dealing with it.'

* * *

Half an hour later, Jack, Bugsy and Velma entered the room and Jack dismissed the uniformed officer guarding the door. He didn't believe Dr Amory was likely to make a run for it and she was hardly a physical threat. He was surprised to see that she was being represented by the duty solicitor and not a smart, expensive lawyer. Then he remembered — she no longer had money.

Velma was operating the recording machine. She switched it on and spoke. 'This interview is being recorded and may be given in evidence if your case is brought to trial. We are in an interview room at Kings Richington police station.' She announced the date and time, then everyone in the room introduced themselves by name and rank so that their voices would be identified on the recording.

Jack began. 'Dr Amory, do you know why you're here?'

'Yes, because you arrested me. Don't you remember?'

He tried again. 'Do you know why you were arrested?'

She looked enquiringly at her solicitor and he nodded. 'I'm assuming it's to do with Violet Dibble's murder.'

'Do you know anything about that?' asked Bugsy.

'Yes, of course. I killed her with a knitting needle. I had no choice.'

'Can you tell us why you had no choice?' asked Jack, surprised at her total lack of emotion or remorse.

Velma was not at all surprised. This was a woman with an antisocial personality disorder — the tepid term for a sociopath. She neither cared about nor understood other people's feelings and had no regard for right and wrong.

Dr Amory looked Jack straight in the eye. 'I had to get rid of Violet because she saw me.'

'Where did she see you?' asked Bugsy.

Dr Amory turned to her solicitor. 'Are they both allowed to question me at once like this?'

He nodded and carried on scribbling notes.

She shrugged. 'Violet saw me leaving the garden centre. She mentioned it quite casually while we were chatting and she was eating her sandwich. She asked if I'd seen anyone who might have killed Luke whilst I was outside. You see, Luke had sent me a message on my phone asking me to meet him in the yard at the back.'

'Did you take Luke's phone?' asked Bugsy.

'Yes, of course. If I hadn't, you'd have found the text, wouldn't you?' Her expression was one of surprise that these police officers were so obtuse.

'What did you do with it?' asked Jack.

'I borrowed an angle grinder from one of the members of the Bricklayers' Guild, then I ground the phone into small pieces and dropped them down the drain. Anyway, Luke said he had something to show me and it was important. I had a suspicion what it was, so I picked up the pruning scissors and took them with me, in case he wouldn't listen to reason. Obviously, I didn't want the CCTV to record me going out there, so I went out of the main door, walked around the building and came in through the side gate, where they kept all the sheds and statues. I checked that there were no people — they were all inside waiting for the choir to sing. After I'd stabbed Luke, I went out through the side gates again and came back in by the main door. Are you following this?'

Jack and Bugsy were both astonished at the matter-of-fact way this woman was describing how she'd carried out two murders as if it were the most natural thing in the world. Perfectly understandable behaviour, as she saw it.

'Yes, we're following,' replied Jack.

'Violet had remarkably sharp wits for an old lady. Too sharp for her own good as it turned out. Anyway, I knew that if she'd mentioned seeing me coming and going when you interviewed her, you wouldn't believe my statement about being with the choir the whole time that Luke was being stabbed. My alibi would be shot.'

'Would you like to explain why you felt you had to stab Luke?' asked Jack.

'Well, I'm assuming you've seen the photograph and the birth records; they were confiscated by that officer in the custody suite. He was my son. Luke Burton, that is — not the officer in the custody suite. He'd been digging and prying through all the records for months until he traced me. The obsessive need to find his birth mother had influenced his entire life. I shouldn't have minded so much if he'd kept quiet about it, but he was planning to broadcast it to the world. Well, I couldn't have that, could I? Can you imagine the harm it would have done to my image? Let alone the number of votes I'd have lost in the mayoral election, when people found out I'd got pregnant by a married man and had an illegitimate baby.'

'But surely that kind of thing doesn't even raise eyebrows these days? You only have to look at the backgrounds of lots of public figures.' Bugsy was struggling to find a credible rationale for her actions.

'You'd be surprised, Sergeant. People make the right liberal noises, pretend to be progressive and free-thinking, but in reality, minds are still as narrow as they ever were. Especially if you're a Doctor of Theology and expected to set a saintly example. No, as I said, I had no choice.'

'Can you tell us about Charlie Snell?' asked Jack. 'Why did he have to die?'

'I've absolutely no idea, except that he took up space and oxygen on a planet already overcrowded with plebs.' She looked blank. 'What has his death got to do with me?'

'Are you saying you weren't responsible for his murder?' Bugsy had hoped Snell was her hat trick and that she'd confess.

'No, of course not. Why would I kill Charlie Snell? He was of absolutely no consequence to me at all.'

After that, there was little more to say. Jack charged her with the murders of Luke Burton and Violet Dibble and left her to make a full statement. Now, it was down to the Crown Prosecution Service.

* * *

Back in the incident room, Bugsy was still astounded at Dr Amory's attitude. 'How can you be that dispassionate about killing two perfectly innocent human beings? DC Dinkley, you're the expert — explain, please, because I don't understand.'

'She's a high-functioning sociopath, Sarge. She can be cruel without feeling guilty about it. Her condition typically uses intelligence, even charm, to control others. Lying for personal gain comes naturally, even a tendency towards physical violence, if that's what it takes to get what she wants.'

'Well, I daresay some of your fellow "shrinks" will deem her unfit to plead because of her personality disorder and she'll spend the rest of her life in a hospital somewhere. Whichever way it goes, she's forfeited her right to freedom.'

'*Freedom's just another word for nothing left to lose,*' quoted Velma.

'Which one of your lot said that?' asked Aled. 'Nietzsche? Freud? Jung?'

'No, it was Kris Kristofferson actually, but you have to admit, he had a point.'

'It's certainly true in Elizabeth Amory's case,' agreed Jack. 'She's lost everything.'

'Imagine,' added Gemma, 'all those years of good works and virtue signalling down the drain.'

'And the good works must have been particularly difficult for Dr Amory, because people with ASPD don't really care about anyone but themselves,' Velma confirmed.

Aled was putting ticks against the photographs of persons on the whiteboard whose murders had been successfully solved, which left information relating to the murder of Charlie Snell. 'Did you believe Dr Amory when she denied any involvement in the Snell murder, sir?'

'Yes, I did,' said Jack. 'Even allowing for her personality disorder, she had nothing to gain by confessing to two murders but denying responsibility for a third.'

'Even though she was the person who discovered the body, like she did Mrs Dibble?' asked Gemma.

'That was always my working hypothesis,' said Bugsy, 'but I agree with the inspector; it wasn't the case with Snell.'

'We still don't have a credible motive for Snell's murder,' said Jack. 'It isn't enough to say he was a nasty piece of work with disgusting habits and nobody liked him. I mean, you could say that about a lot of blokes.'

'I hope you're not looking at me, guv,' said Bugsy. 'I don't keep mouldy pasties in my pocket anymore, Carlene made me give up smoking and Iris makes me change my socks every day.'

'The NCA guys are convinced that he wasn't eliminated by the passport gang, so who else wanted him dead?' Jack asked.

'Just off the top of my head, how about some butcher he put out of business by selling cheap, substandard meat,' offered Aled.

'I know it's unlikely given the type of man he was, but there may have been some misguided woman he was dallying with whose husband decided to put a stop to it,' Gemma suggested. 'We know Mrs Snell said he was an inveterate skirt-chaser. Perhaps he had arranged an assignation in the woods and her husband turned up instead.'

'Or blackmailing someone he'd bought a passport from and threatening them,' added Velma.

'Speaking of the passport gang, sir,' called someone from the back of the room, 'how is Chippy? Can we visit yet?'

'Yes, the medics say he is well enough to receive visitors. However, his mother has moved him to a private hospital and she guards him like a rottweiler. Police officers in particular are definitely persona non grata.'

'When will he be coming back, sir?' asked someone else.

'I'm not at all sure that he will. His mother wants to take him home to New Zealand.'

There were noisy protests. 'She can't do that,' declared Aled. 'Being a detective in the MIT is all he's ever wanted to do.'

'And he's good at it,' said Gemma. 'He'll have learned that sometimes discretion is the better part of valour and he won't make the same mistake again. You can't let her just take him away, sir. Can't you persuade her?'

'Gemma, I've been trying for years to persuade my wife that discretion is safer than valour with dismal results, but

I agree, it would be a great shame to lose DC Chippendale from the team. When he's a bit more robust, I suggest we visit mob-handed and demonstrate our support.'

* * *

The report in the *Echo* read:

> *Dr Elizabeth Grace Amory, well-known for her prolific community work and an active member of the Richington Community Choir, attended the magistrates' court hearing today, charged with the murders of Luke Burton, 25, and Violet Dibble, 84, who were also members of the choir. Dr Amory pleaded not guilty due to diminished responsibility. Based on the seriousness of the offences, the case was referred for reports and subsequent trial in the Crown Court.*

The editor of the *Echo* had sent his best crime reporter to the magistrates' court for Elizabeth Amory's first hearing as she was a prominent member of the community and would generate a lot of public interest. Predictably, bail was refused, and the serious indictable offence of double murder was referred for trial in the Crown Court. As Bugsy had anticipated, Amory's counsel offered a plea of diminished responsibility due to a personality disorder. However, the report of the forensic psychologists, after several face-to-face assessments, disagreed.

The editor was aware that some members of the Richington community regarded Dr Amory as a paragon of virtue and a force for good, believing her actions were inspired by a genuine concern for others. Of course, that was exactly how she wanted to be perceived, expecting them to show their gratitude at the polls. However, she had subjected his editorials to blistering criticism on several occasions in the past, and in simple terms, he regarded her as a 'blasted nuisance'. Now it turned out she had been a 'dangerous nuisance' and it was his duty, he decided, to maintain objectivity in journalism, and to present the unbiased facts. With that in mind and given that it was permissible for such information to be shared among agencies such as the press, in order to safeguard public interest, he obtained and published the forensic psychologist's summary report, word for word.

> *Dr Amory understands the concept of right and wrong, at least on an intellectual level, but she refuses to live by it. She has no empathy, is pathologically dishonest and has gone through life using manipulation, intimidation and often violence to achieve her aims. She is incapable of feeling guilt. She knew what she was doing but did it anyway because that is who she is. She hid the crimes she committed so she could continue to do what she chose to do. This proves she is fit to plead in the legal sense. She does not have judicial immunity.*

CHAPTER FOURTEEN

Bryn Thomas swaggered across the forecourt of Smart's Autos with his hands in his pockets and began sauntering amongst the cars, kicking tyres and trying the doors.

Reluctantly, Geoff Smart went out to speak to him. A sale was a sale, even if the customer was a pompous prick. He attempted a welcoming smile. 'Bryn, what brings you here?'

'Well, I haven't come to buy a pound of spuds, have I?' His tone was mocking. 'I want a new car. Mine's starting to pack up. I need something that will get me to a music festival in North Wales.'

'That sounds very . . . er . . . interesting. Is Fliss going with you?' Geoff thought probably not, and he was right.

'Of course not. What would be the point of taking Felicity? She doesn't appreciate good music, and she doesn't speak Welsh. It would be like showing a dog a card trick — a completely wasted exercise. Added to which, she'd be an infernal nuisance, following me around to see who I was talking to and wanting attention all the time. No, I'm leaving her at home.'

Geoff fought the urge to smack Bryn in the mouth. 'What kind of car did you have in mind? This one's a nice little runner.' He indicated a small saloon.

'No, I want something smarter than that. What about that one over there?' Bryn pointed to a nearly new luxury convertible.

'Well, of course, that's a first-rate car but probably way out of your price range.'

'Don't worry, I can afford it,' he boasted.

Geoff laughed with more than a hint of scorn. 'Have you won the lottery or something?'

'No. It's a present from my wife, only she doesn't know it yet.' He smirked unpleasantly.

They went across and Bryn spent some time sitting in the car, examining the instruments and controls and working the soft-top roof. 'Yes, I think I'll take this one. Does it have that satnav gadget? Only I'm not sure of the route once I leave the main drag and I find maps totally incomprehensible.'

'Yes, of course it does. A car of this quality has excellent satnav. Not only can you select the destination, but it also lets you determine which elements of the route to follow or avoid.'

'Good. I'll pick it up at the weekend after I've sorted the insurance.'

They completed the paperwork and bank transfer, then Bryn strolled back to his old car, whistling.

Half an hour later, a police car drew up and two detectives in plain clothes climbed out. Geoff recognized the tall one with the crooked nose from the garden centre. He'd been in charge when Luke Burton had been killed. The short, fat one was his sidekick. He watched them walk towards the office and wondered what they wanted. 'Good afternoon, gentlemen. How can I help?'

Jack and Bugsy produced their warrant cards. 'May we have a word, Mr Smart?'

'Yes, of course. Please come in. Can I get you anything — tea? Coffee?'

'No, thank you, sir,' said Jack. 'We're making enquiries about the death of Charlie Snell.'

'You detectives have certainly had your work cut out recently,' said Geoff. 'First Snell, then Luke and poor Violet.

I saw the article in the *Echo*. Who'd have thought the pious Elizabeth Amory was a murderer? I was gobsmacked, I don't mind telling you. Not so much when I read about old Julian Amory shooting himself, though. The way he gambled was off the charts. I mean, he'd bet a grand on two drops of rain running down the window. He must have gone through thousands before it finally caught up with him. But you're here to talk about Charlie. Nasty piece of work.'

'So everyone keeps telling us, sir,' said Bugsy. 'But we still need to find and arrest whoever killed him.'

'Yes, of course you do. I'm guessing you don't have Dr Amory in the frame for that one, too?'

'No, sir,' confirmed Bugsy.

'OK, so how do you think I can help?'

'We're asking people who knew Snell if they could give us any additional information as to who might want him dead, apart from the usual "nobody liked him",' said Jack.

'I guess you know about his blackmail hustle.' Geoff could see from their faces that they didn't.

Jack and Bugsy exchanged glances. 'No, Mr Smart, we don't. Can you tell us about that?'

'As well as his other dodgy activities, Snell made it his business to use his butcher's shop to encourage customers, usually ladies, to tell him personal incriminating stuff about themselves and their neighbours. You know how communities like to gossip. Then he demanded money from the victims to keep quiet. Like I said, he was a nasty piece of work.'

'Do you know who any of these people are?' asked Bugsy hopefully.

'No, not really. Obviously people paid him to stay silent, so it wasn't likely to become common knowledge, was it? But I do know he tried it on with Bryn Thomas. He found out somehow that Bryn had done time and threatened to broadcast it. Well, you know how pompous and self-important Bryn is, so that was the last thing he wanted.'

'Do you know if Mr Thomas paid him any money?' asked Jack.

'No. I'm afraid I don't, but I doubt it. He was more likely to try and shut him up than give him money.'

'Well, thank you, that's very helpful.' They turned to go, then Bugsy asked, 'Might we ask how you came by this information, sir?'

'Gallantry precludes me from disclosing my sources, gentlemen. You'll just have to take my word for it. Or you could always ask Bryn himself, of course.'

'What do you suppose he meant by gallantry precluding him from telling us, Bugsy?' Jack asked once they were out of earshot.

'I'm guessing he meant that he got the information from Roxy Wild. Aled said Smart hinted that they hooked up occasionally.'

Jack was puzzled. 'What does "hooked up" mean?'

'It means casual sex without being in a committed relationship, guv. Back in the day, we used to call it a "one-night stand".'

'You speak for yourself, Sergeant. I'd be on a permanent diet of kale and kimchi if Corrie thought I'd done anything like that.'

* * *

Back at the station, Jack shared the blackmail information with the rest of the team.

'Blimey!' exclaimed Aled. 'Was there any swindle that Charlie Snell wasn't involved in? The man was a walking crime sheet.'

'Now that we know he was a blackmailer, it puts a whole lot more suspects in the frame as his killer,' Gemma decided.

'It also explains why he had so much cash,' said Clive. 'Blackmail victims don't pay hush money using their credit cards.'

'Clive, did we find anything useful on Snell's phone that might give us the names of some of his victims?' asked Jack.

Clive went back through his searches. 'No, sir. All his calls were legitimate. I guess he'd have had a burner phone for his illegal activities and it doesn't look as if SOCOs or Mrs Snell found it.'

'In that case, I think we should pay Bryn Thomas another visit,' said Jack.

* * *

'What is it now?' Bryn Thomas snapped irritably when Jack and Bugsy appeared on the doorstep.

'May we come in, sir?' asked Bugsy.

'Must you? I'm planning a trip to Wales, and I need to prepare.'

'We could do this down at the station if you prefer,' threatened Jack.

Bryn backed down. 'Oh, all right. You'd better come in, but make it quick. I need to go through my music.'

'We've received information that Charlie Snell was attempting to blackmail you with regard to your time in prison,' began Bugsy.

'Who told you that? Was it my wife?'

'Why should you think that, sir?' asked Bugsy.

'Because apart from Snell himself, she was the only one who knew about his filthy threats. She had no business discussing it with the police.' He was starting to go red in the face with temper.

'Was that why you killed him, Mr Thomas?' Jack probed.

'What? No, of course I didn't kill him. I didn't have to — he was already . . .'

'Already what? Already dead?' Bugsy prompted.

Thomas sank onto a chair, pomposity temporarily punctured. 'Yes, if you must know. I had arranged to meet him in Richington Forest after choir practice. Neither of us wanted to be seen conducting any kind of transaction in the church hall in front of the others. He thought I was just going to meekly hand over the money, but I intended to teach him a lesson. It was dark and raining hard. I got lost looking for the meeting place and when I eventually found it, he was lying there, dead. There, now you have it, so leave me alone.'

'Why didn't you report it?' asked Jack, showing no inclination to leave.

'Why do you think? Because you would have immediately fitted me up for his murder, like you tried to just now. I'm not stupid!'

'Did you see anybody else in the forest?' asked Bugsy.

'No, I didn't. I wasn't going to hang around — I went to the pub for a stiff drink then I went home.'

'So you lied in your statement when you said you and Mrs Thomas went straight home to bed after choir practice?'

'Yes. Are you going to arrest me?'

'Not yet, sir,' said Jack. 'But don't leave Kings Richington without telling the police.' They moved towards the door.

'But what about my trip to Wales?'

'We'll let you know.' They saw themselves out.

* * *

'What did you make of that, Bugsy?' They were driving back to the station.

'I don't believe he's our killer, guv. Like most bullies, he's full of bluff and bullshit but no balls.'

'I agree. But it explains the fourth set of footprints SOCOs found on the edge of the clearing. Thomas stood there long enough to see that Snell was dead and then legged it.'

'Of course, now that he doesn't have an alibi for the time Snell was killed, neither does his wife,' said Bugsy.

'True,' agreed Jack. 'Although, the smart money is that the killer was one of his blackmail victims. But how do we find out who and how many there were? We can hardly put an advert in the *Echo* asking them to come forward.'

'Whoever they are, they'll just be thankful he's dead and the demands for money have stopped,' said Bugsy. 'If it were me, I'd keep schtum.'

Jack frowned. 'It's a tricky one with little to go on, and we're no further forward than when it happened.'

'Look on the bright side, guv. This time last week we had three unsolved murders, now we only have one — two out of three isn't bad.'

'I don't imagine Garwood will see it like that.'

'What about Roxy Wild? Didn't Mrs Snell suspect Charlie of chasing after her? Maybe she knows something about the blackmail. Why don't we go and ask her?'

'If I didn't know you better, Bugsy, I'd suspect you of wanting to take a closer look at her merchandise.'

'Not at all. It's just that it's Iris's birthday next week and I'm stuck for ideas for a present. I thought I'd get some inspiration from Wild Styles.'

* * *

The shop was busy when they arrived and they kept a low profile until Roxy had finished serving. She came round to the other side of the counter to meet them. 'It's Inspector Dawes and Sergeant Malone, isn't it?'

'That's right Madam,' said Bugsy. 'I wonder if we might have a word?'

'Yes, of course. I remember you from that ghastly time at the garden centre when poor Luke was found dead. Who'd have believed Busy Lizzie was his mother and she killed him to shut him up? What kind of woman would do that? And then poor old Violet, too. I tell you, I shouldn't have thought it possible if I hadn't seen it in print in the *Echo*. Not that I ever believed that sanctimonious act of hers. Elizabeth Amory was an evil bitch — pardon my French.'

'Actually, we're here to ask you about Charlie Snell,' began Jack, hoping to divert her from the character assassination.

She pulled a face. 'He was another menace that Kings Richington is better off without.'

'Why do you say that, Madam?'

'Please stop calling me Madam, Sergeant Malone. It makes me sound like I'm running a knocking shop. Call me Roxy.'

'OK, Roxy. What was it that you didn't like about Charlie Snell?'

She decided this was a good time to tell them about what she'd heard at Smart's Autos. 'I overheard him fighting with Geoff Smart. I don't know what it was about, so don't ask me, but it must have been something bad because I heard Geoff say, "I know what you're up to, Snell, and you can pack it in or you'll be sorry." Then there was the sound of punches and things falling over and breaking.'

'What happened after that?' asked Jack.

'I don't know. I didn't stick around to find out.'

'We have information that Snell was a blackmailer,' added Jack. 'Do you think that's what Mr Smart meant?'

'I wouldn't like to hazard a guess, but one thing I do know, Geoff's a good bloke. Giving Charlie a beating is the most he'd do — he wouldn't have killed him.'

'Well . . . er . . . thank you, Roxy,' said Jack. 'Before we leave, my sergeant here is looking for a birthday present for his wife.'

'You've come to the right place, Sergeant.' She lapsed instantly into sales mode. 'What did you have in mind? A matching bra and panties set? A see-through nightie? What's her favourite colour?'

'Erm . . . pink, I think.'

'How about these?' Roxy held up a pink lace string thong and matching plunge bra. 'And as a special birthday treat, how about a toy? I have a pretty pink love rabbit with vibrating ears.'

'I think she's too grown up for a toy rabbit,' said Bugsy, wondering why its ears vibrated.

'Not for this one, she isn't.' Roxy took it out of the box and showed him. 'It has three speeds and ten vibration patterns. Guaranteed hours of fun.'

Bugsy gulped. Despite his time in the vice squad, he'd never seen one before. 'Oh . . . er . . . no, thanks. I don't think . . . I mean . . . she wouldn't . . . she doesn't . . . I'll . . . er . . . just take the bra and knickers, thank you.'

'How about you, Inspector? Since you're here, I'm sure your lovely wife would be thrilled with some new sexy lingerie.'

Such was Roxy's sales technique and her well-practised powers of persuasion, both police officers left with a set of highly inappropriate and very expensive underwear for their wives.

* * *

Bryn was feeling liberated. Now that he no longer had to work, he could concentrate on the things that really mattered. He realized he should have given up the stupid job a long time ago. After all, he didn't need the money as long as he had access to Felicity's. First on his bucket list was the music festival in North Wales. The venue was close to the village where he'd been born and brought up. He was looking forward to seeing it again after all these years. He had packed enough clothes to last for a couple of weeks, but he was seriously considering staying longer. Maybe he wouldn't come back at all. He could still access Felicity's money, and later on, he could put the house up for sale, as it was in his name. All sorts of possibilities lay ahead, even an attractive new partner. Not that Felicity had ever been much of a partner — they had little in common. In fact, he couldn't remember what it was he'd seen in her. She had no personality and it certainly wasn't her looks that had attracted him. Of course, her parents' money could have had something to do with it.

He went up to his room to dress in the clothes he had set aside for the journey. He'd chosen an outfit to match his new free-spirited aesthetic — a bold printed tunic over baggy denims, cowboy boots and a black fedora. He looked at himself in the full-length mirror. Perfect. Just the right combination of boho-chic and festival freedom. He had a sudden thought. His shoulder-length hair would fly about in the convertible. He took off the hat and twisted his hair up into a man bun. Even better. Now he just needed a bead necklace, a few cord bracelets and his shades and he was ready. He'd wanted to take his jacket with the Welsh dragon logo on the back, but he couldn't find it. No doubt Felicity had tidied it away somewhere. She was always moving his belongings. On the other hand, he might have left it in the church hall. No matter, he'd buy himself a new one when he got there. He had no idea whereabouts in the rambling old house Felicity had disappeared to, but he saw no need to say goodbye or tell her how long he'd be away.

He drove his old car to Smart's garage and abandoned it in a corner of the forecourt, then went to the office to pick up the keys to his stylish new convertible. The sun was glinting off the metallic silver finish, making it appear even more opulent.

Geoff looked him up and down, taking in the floral tunic, cowboy boots and hat. 'Dear God, man, what have you come as? You never said this festival was fancy dress. Who are you meant to be? Widow Twankey or Butch Cassidy?'

'Never mind the cracks, Smart. I need you to show me how the satnav thingy works on my car. I'm going to need it, because I'm not sure of the route. The last time I was there, I wasn't old enough to drive.' They went out to the convertible and Bryn climbed into the driving seat.

Geoff got in beside him and pressed a few buttons on the slick touchscreen control panel. 'Give me the post code.'

'I don't have the post code. Only the name of the place where the festival is going to be held.'

'Well, give me that, then!' Geoff was losing patience with this dreadful man.

'Aberfechan Bay. It's a seaside town on the north coast, with cliffs overlooking the sea.'

'There you are,' said Geoff, several minutes later. 'I've programmed it. Just keep driving wherever it sends you. Don't argue with it and don't leave the route or you'll get lost. Do you understand? Don't leave the route under any circumstances.' He climbed out. Bryn started the engine and made off without so much as a backward glance.

Geoff went back into the office, picked up his phone and pressed a speed key. 'Fliss, it's me. He's gone. I'm coming over.'

* * *

The black cherry rolled off the kitchen table and made one final desperate bid for freedom before Iris grabbed it and disembowelled it, ready for bottling. 'I'm so glad of your help with these cherries, ladies. We had such a glut on the trees this year. This would have taken me months on my own.'

Iris, Cynthia and Carlene were sitting around Corrie's kitchen table in front of a huge pile of cherries, painstakingly removing the stalks and stones. They each had a large glass of wine and some nibbles to help with the process, and they were putting the world to rights.

'What did you guys think about the saintly Elizabeth Amory?' asked Carlene. She pitted a cherry then popped it in her mouth. 'It's all over social media.'

'Well, I never liked her,' said Cynthia, 'but I never thought she was capable of murder. George is just relieved Jack and the team cracked it before the bigwigs started asking difficult questions. Most of them were friends of the Amorys, so it must have been awkward when they turned out to be criminals. Julian took the easy way out.'

'Poor Violet,' said Corrie. 'She was a sweet old lady. What a ghastly way to go. And young Luke Burton. The *Echo* said he was Busy Lizzie's son.'

'How could she do that to her own flesh and blood?' Iris was thinking of her own son, Dan Griffin, a GP and much-loved father of her two grandchildren. Both she and Bugsy doted on them. 'It's inconceivable.'

'They still haven't got anybody for the Charlie Snell murder,' observed Corrie. 'There are so many people with a possible motive they're spoiled for choice. At the moment, the theory is that it was someone he was blackmailing and they decided to put a stop to it.'

'My money's on his wife,' announced Cynthia.

'What evidence do you have for that outrageous suggestion?' Corrie challenged her.

'I don't need evidence.' Cynthia held out her glass for a top-up. 'You show me a married couple — any married couple — and I'll show you a woman who, at some point, has had to resist the urge to bash her husband over the head with something hefty. It's human nature. Husbands can be bloody irritating.' She took a good glug of wine. 'I bet if we looked at the statistics, a large percentage of married men will have spent time in A&E with concussion.'

'I agree,' said Iris, with feeling.

'Speaking of husbands,' said Corrie, detecting frosty marital hostility in the Malone household, 'what did Bugsy give you for your birthday, Iris?'

Wordlessly, Iris took out her phone, pulled up an image of the offending garments and passed it around.

'I don't believe it!' Corrie was suppressing giggles.

'Does anybody really find that stuff sexy?' asked Carlene. 'Apart from dirty old men in raincoats.'

'You do realize, don't you, Iris . . .?' Cynthia was on her third very large glass of Chardonnay on an empty stomach, with only nibbles to soak it up. Her speech was becoming a little slurred. She leaned across and patted Iris's arm in a gesture of feminine solidarity. 'You do realize . . . that when husbands buy you a present like that, they really buy it for *themselves*. What they want is for you to put them on and parade around in them, like a sleazy strip show. You didn't do that, did you?'

'Certainly not!' Iris was emphatic. 'For a start, they were a size ten and I'm the wrong side of a sixteen. I put them back in the pink cutesy bag, tied it up with the pink satin ribbon — then I threw it at his head!'

'Attagirl, Iris!' they chorused and drank a toast to her, clinking their glasses.

'Hey, ladies.' Jack emerged from the hall, having just come in after a long day at the station. He kissed Corrie on the cheek. 'Who are you toasting?'

'Iris,' answered Corrie. 'You'll never believe this. Bugsy gave her a frightful bra and thong set that belongs in a porno mag for her birthday. She was so disgusted she threw them at him. Can you credit that?'

Jack swiftly whisked the bag he was holding behind his back. 'Er . . . no, that doesn't sound like Bugsy at all. He must have been talked into it by the salesperson.'

'You wouldn't ever buy me anything like that, would you?' Corrie wondered.

'No, no, not at all, my love. Of course I wouldn't. I'm . . . er . . . just going for a shower.' He turned to hurry off.

'What's in the bag, darling?' asked Corrie.

'This? Oh, nothing. I was just clearing out the glove compartment of the car. It's rubbish. I'll put it in the wheelie bin.' He dashed out before things got any worse.

CHAPTER FIFTEEN

Bryn followed the satnav's fastest route without deviation, as Geoff Smart had instructed. It took him north from Kings Richington, skirting around Oxford and Birmingham before travelling west into North Wales. He knew he was looking at a good six hours of driving and it would be dark by the time he reached Aberfechan Bay. He wasn't worried. The car was going like a dream, and he didn't intend to stop until he got there. A sumptuous dinner awaited him when he reached the luxury hotel he'd booked. None of that primitive festival camping nonsense. He wasn't twenty any longer and he didn't intend to rough it in two feet of mud.

All went well until the storm set in. He stopped and put up the soft-top. By the time he reached Shrewsbury, visibility had diminished drastically until he wondered if he should pull over somewhere, but he decided against it. The lights and windscreen wipers on the car were good and he was looking forward to dinner and a hot bath in the five-star hotel. No point wasting time in some rough-and-ready place, even if he could find one. He'd push on, following the satnav.

Some hours later, the weather had worsened and Bryn was starting to feel tired. The satnav told him he was nearing Aberfechan Bay, so he shook himself awake, drank some water and turned on the radio. Classic FM was playing extracts from Wagner's *Ring Cycle* by the Vienna Philharmonic. *That should keep me awake*, he thought. Not much longer and he'd be relaxing in the luxury penthouse suite he'd booked.

Gradually, the road began to narrow. He pressed on, remembering what Smart had said about not leaving the route or he'd get lost. The thought of losing his way at night, in unknown territory and in this weather, was not a good one. A blinding flash of lightning was followed by a deafening crash of thunder and then the rain poured down, hitting the windscreen like bullets. Fittingly, 'The Ride of the Valkyries' blasted from the radio, evoking the Norse myth of warrior women on horseback, scooping up the slain from the battlefield and carrying their souls into Valhalla.

Soon, he was skidding down a steep, narrow pathway. The satnav kept insisting the path was a road, even though it was getting narrower and steeper, but he trusted the directions and kept going, his knuckles white from gripping the wheel. He only realized something was wrong when the car hit a fence. It ploughed through, and with the Valkyries drowning Bryn's screams, the car plummeted two hundred feet over the cliffs and came to rest upside down in the sea.

* * *

The editor of the *Richington Echo* had received a report from an old friend and colleague, now working on the *Aberfechan Chronicle*. The accompanying email informed him that he might be interested as the police had identified the owner from the car's plates. It was Bryn Thomas from Kings Richington. The *Chronicle*'s report read:

> *A car has landed upside down in the Irish Sea, having been driven off the cliff above Aberfechan Beach at a spot known as Devil's Drop. The bizarre incident was discovered during the early hours of Friday morning. A spokesperson for the coastguard said: We were paged to assist North Wales*

Police with a vehicle that was submerged in the sea at high tide. Fire and Rescue teams were on hand and a helicopter was deployed to winch the vehicle out. It is thought that the single occupant, Mr Bryn Thomas from Kings Richington, England, was killed instantly. His identity has yet to be formally confirmed.

At about the same time, Kings Richington Police received a similar report from the North Wales Police requesting them to contact the next of kin. In view of the recent deaths of the choir members associated with Bryn Thomas, Commander Sir Barnaby Featherstonehaugh decided the follow-up should be delegated to the Murder Investigation Team and, as such, it landed on DCS Garwood's desk, or rather, on his computer. Garwood was a firm believer that 'excrement rolls downhill' or words to that effect, and passed it down to Jack, instructing him to find out whether there was more to it than an unfortunate driving accident. Any more deaths, even remotely associated to the Richington Community Choir, were to be treated as sensitive. He had already been hauled over the coals by the Commander regarding what he termed 'unnecessarily sensational media coverage' of the three murders and the suicide that had already occurred, one of which, Charlie Snell, was still outstanding. Sir Barnaby and Lady Lobelia had been close acquaintances of Julian and Elizabeth Amory; they had even been on holiday together, but they were now anxious to distance themselves from the scandal. The Commander's exact order had been, 'Pull your finger out, Garwood! Clear up this mess!'

* * *

'Four murders and a suicide,' quipped Aled, pinning another photograph of a live person, now dead, to the whiteboard.

'Except this is real life, not a romcom,' chastised Gemma. 'And anyway, Bryn Thomas's death looks like an accident, not a murder. And before anyone suggests it, he was definitely not the kind of man to commit suicide. Much too arrogant.'

'You have to admit it's a bit spooky though,' continued Aled. 'All of them had some connection to the Richington Choir. Do you think there'll be any more, sir?'

'I sincerely hope not . . . but until the case is closed, all bets are off,' said Jack. 'The Chief Super is already eating his own weight in indigestion tablets. Right now, Sergeant Malone and I have the unenviable task of visiting Felicity Thomas and explaining how her husband died. Gemma, you're on tea and tissues duty.'

As it turned out, there was no need for the tissues. When they knocked on the door of the big Edwardian house, it was answered by a chipper Felicity looking far from heartbroken. She smiled a welcome. 'Please come in. I'm guessing you're here about Bryn.'

'That's right, Mrs Thomas,' replied Bugsy. 'We're very sorry for your loss.'

'Thank you. That's very kind.'

'How did you hear about Mr Thomas's accident?' asked Jack.

'Such news travels fast, Inspector. Bryn had relatives in Wales. They read the report in the local paper, watched it on the television news and phoned me. Would you like some tea?'

'It's all right, Mrs Thomas,' said Gemma. 'I'll make it.' After several attempts, wandering down draughty corridors, she found the Edwardian kitchen. It had a huge oak dresser almost filling one wall, a quarry-tiled floor and a solid fuel cooker. Copper pans and jugs hung from a rack attached to the ceiling along with various dried flowers and herbs. The room could have been a colour plate from an Edwardian homes and gardens magazine. She filled the kettle and put it on the hotplate to boil. It was while she was waiting that something caught her attention in the mature, overgrown garden. She made a mental note to mention it to the inspector but not yet. Experience told her that this would not be a good time.

'We know that your husband was on his way to a music festival in Wales, Mrs Thomas. He mentioned it the last time we spoke. But you didn't go with him. Why was that?'

'Welsh festivals, Eisteddfods and the like, aren't really my scene. And as it turned out, it was lucky I didn't go, otherwise I'd have gone over the cliff with him, wouldn't I?' She was quite pragmatic with no emotion.

'Yes, quite.' Jack paused. 'I understand from the Welsh police that he had only recently acquired the car he was driving.'

'That's right. He got it from Smart's Autos on the bypass. He felt he needed something more modern. It's a long way to North Wales and his old vehicle wasn't altogether reliable.'

Gemma came in with a tea tray and handed round mugs.

'Oh, thank you, dear,' Felicity gushed. 'I think I've got some rock buns somewhere. Would anybody like one?'

'No, thank you, Mrs Thomas. We're fine.' Jack had heard about the infamous rock buns from Aled. 'It appears from the Welsh authorities that your husband's death was a tragic accident.'

She looked surprised. 'What else would it be?'

'Is there any possibility that your husband might have committed suicide?' ventured Jack.

'Absolutely not!' Her reply was spontaneous. 'Bryn loved his life. Why wouldn't he? He did exactly what he wanted, when he wanted, without recourse to anyone. Like going off on this trip alone. Why would he commit suicide?'

No doubt she's thinking of the life insurance, thought Bugsy, whose instinct was always to follow the money. 'Was Bryn a good driver?' he asked.

'Yes, most of the time, but it was an unfamiliar car. He wasn't used to it. He must have lost control. Maybe he stood on the accelerator instead of the brake. We'll never know, will we?'

'The car, and Mr Thomas's body, are being brought back to Kings Richington so the police engineers and the pathologist can examine them here. We need to be sure that there was nothing amiss with the car. You'll be needed to identify the body formally, Mrs Thomas. Will you be all right with that?' Jack watched her reaction.

'Er . . . yes, I suppose so.' She sounded less than confident for the first time. 'How soon will that be? Only I have a lot of formalities to attend to and a funeral to arrange, and after that, I was hoping to go away for a holiday, just to get over the shock.'

'We'll try to get everything dealt with as quickly as possible.' Jack and Bugsy stood up to leave. 'We'll be in touch. Goodbye, Mrs Thomas.'

In the car driving back to the station, Gemma reported what she'd seen. 'Sir, while I was in the kitchen making tea, I happened to glance out of the window and I saw Geoff Smart climbing over the hedge at the bottom of the garden.'

'Did you indeed?' said Jack. 'Are you sure it was him?'

'Positive, sir. I recognized him from his photo on the whiteboard.'

'Are you thinking what I'm thinking, guv?' asked Bugsy.

'Geoff Smart and Felicity Thomas are an item. Smart sold Thomas a dodgy car having tampered with the brakes to get rid of him.'

'But wouldn't Thomas have noticed something wrong with his brakes before he got there, Sarge?' asked Gemma. 'He'd already driven over two hundred miles.'

'Not if they only failed when he was skidding down the steep path to Devil's Drop in the storm.'

'I guess it's possible,' said Jack. 'I don't know anything about the workings of cars — especially modern ones. We'll wait until the lads in the garage have taken it apart, then we'll talk to Smart.'

* * *

It was some time before the car and the body were available for examination in Kings Richington. In the police garage, mechanics took what was left of the car apart and tested every component, down to the last nut and bolt. Jack and Bugsy were invited for a verbal update.

'Obviously the car took a beating bouncing off the cliffs and into the sea, but before that, as far as we can tell, it was in perfect working order.' The chief engineer wiped her hands on an oily rag. 'It was a first-rate vehicle. Such a waste.'

'Anything wrong with the brakes?' asked Jack hopefully.

'Nothing that my mechanics could find, and believe me, if there had been any sabotage, they'd have found it. It's what they're trained for.'

'So there's nothing that could indicate anything other than an unfortunate accident in bad weather?' asked Bugsy.

'No, Sergeant. And although the seat belt had smashed loose from its moorings, from what we could see from the webbing, the driver had been wearing it at the time of impact.' She paused. 'Why? Were you suspecting foul play of some kind?'

For a fleeting moment that he rapidly dismissed, Bugsy wondered if he dared ask her to take a look at his step-grandson James's bike. Since he had 'mended' it, a wheel had buckled and the chain slipped off whenever the lad pedalled hard. Bugsy was beginning to think it would be safer if he just bought him a new bike.

'We needed to be sure that the car hadn't been tampered with, that's all,' replied Jack. 'Thank you very much for your help.'

'Not at all, Inspector.' She gave him a cheery smile. 'You'll get my full report in a day or two, or maybe three. Cars I can handle — reports not so much.'

Outside, Bugsy shrugged. 'Well, that's knocked that theory on the head, guv. I felt sure Smart had done something to the car. It's too much of a coincidence that the bloke who was having it off with Thomas's wife also supplied him with the car that killed him.'

'Yes, and you know what I think of coincidences,' said Jack. He looked at his watch. 'We need to be at the mortuary. Dr Hardacre will have finished the post-mortem on Thomas's body by now.'

* * *

Dr Hardacre had finished examining Thomas's battered corpse when they arrived. She peeled off the latex gloves and handed them to Miss Catwater, who disposed of them in the bin, then hurried off to prepare the next cadaver for examination.

'OK, Doc, what was it? Drink, drugs or a massive stroke?' Bugsy asked.

'The tox report didn't find any traces of alcohol or drugs in his blood and there was no water in his lungs, so he didn't drown. Nor is there evidence of cardiac arrest, a stroke or anything else that would have stopped him in his tracks.'

'So what killed him?' Bugsy knew as soon as he asked that it was what Big Ron would deem 'a bloody silly question', and as such, it would earn him one of her caustic answers. He braced himself.

She gave him a penetrating stare. 'Of course, I'm no expert, Sergeant, and I've only been a pathologist for twenty years, so this is purely a guess, you understand, but I think it may have had something to do with plunging two hundred feet off a cliff into the sea.'

'Obviously, nobody would survive that, Doc.' Bugsy was apologetic.

Jack smiled to himself. Poor Bugsy always managed to put his foot in it where the pathologist was involved.

She continued in a more helpful vein. 'In these circumstances, bodies are like wasps being shaken up in a jar,' she explained. 'Not only did this man hit objects whilst being chucked around inside the car, but his internal organs were also smashed around, getting torn, crushed, separated and pierced during the impact of the vehicle against the cliffs. The fact that the car had a soft-top didn't help to protect him. Most of his bones were broken and much of his soft tissue was compressed into a pulp. But if you're looking for evidence of another murder, Inspector, I can't help you.'

They left Dr Hardacre preparing Thomas for identification and went back to the station. 'OK, team.' Jack explained the results of the tests. 'The car wasn't sabotaged, and Thomas wasn't stoned or drunk and he didn't suffer a cardiac incident. Where do we go from here?'

'We may have to accept that we'll never know what made him drive over the cliff,' said Aled. 'We could speculate all day.'

'Our death rate hasn't half gone up recently,' commented one of the support team, peering at the photos on the whiteboard. 'That's five now, sir.'

There were murmurs of agreement around the room.

'Thanks for reminding me,' said Jack grimly.

'There is just one thing left we could check, sir.' Clive was frowning, ready to go delving.

Jack knew that look. It was hard to tell what was going on in the brain of a digital forensic specialist at the best of times, but in Clive's case, it was usually something obscure but inspired. This was no exception.

'When the mechanics took the remains of the car apart, I wonder if they managed to salvage the MicroSD card from the satnav system. It would have been in the slot beneath the audio control panel in the centre console. I ask because I might be able to track the last destination that Thomas had programmed into it. If nothing else, it might explain why he ended up where he did instead of Aberfechan village.'

'Won't the sea water have corrupted it?' asked Bugsy.

'Not necessarily. It wasn't in there long enough. It's worth a try. If I can get hold of it, I'll dry it out and see what's on it.'

* * *

Bugsy approached the front door of his modest semi with trepidation. He would have thrown his hat in first, only he didn't wear one. The massive bouquet of flowers he was carrying was, he believed, proportionate to the marital crime he had unintentionally committed. Marrying late in life, as a crusty old bachelor, did not prepare you for all the booby traps and pitfalls that trip you up without you even seeing them coming. The carrier bag on his arm contained a large bottle of Iris's favourite perfume and in his pocket were tickets for her favourite musical, currently on at a West End theatre. If they didn't put things right, he guessed the last resort would be to move into the garden shed. Marrying Iris was the best thing that had ever happened to him. The thought of losing her love and support through his own stupid tactlessness was unbearable.

There was only one way to approach this, he decided. Abject and total mortification. The old sackcloth and ashes ploy. He'd throw himself upon her mercy. As it turned out, that wasn't all he threw himself upon. Hindered by the enormous bouquet in his arms, he pushed open the kitchen door just as Iris pulled it from the other side. He catapulted in, tripped over the cat and knocked himself out on the edge of the sink. When he came round, he was lying on the chequered vinyl flooring with Iris crouched over him, anxiously calling his name.

'Mike, my darling, are you OK? Speak to me — please.' Iris was one of the few people who called Bugsy by his proper name.

After the stars stopped exploding in his head, his first instinct was to look for the bag he'd been carrying. He sat up, grabbed it and felt inside. 'Oh thank goodness. It isn't broken.' He offered it to her. 'Here you are, sweetheart. Your favourite perfume. Happy belated birthday. I'm so sorry for the ... er ... other stuff. I wasn't thinking straight.'

'Should I call an ambulance?' Iris was distraught.

'No, love, I'll be fine. Bit of a headache, that's all.'

'But you're bleeding from a cut on your head. I'll get the first aid kit.'

Bugsy eased his bulk off the floor and onto a kitchen chair while she ministered to him.

'You're going to have a huge lump by tomorrow and probably a black eye, too. Shall I get you some paracetamols?'

'I'd rather have a nice cup of tea and a slice of your fruit cake. Am I forgiven?'

'Of course you are.' She kissed him. 'Marriage at our age isn't always easy, but at least we're in it together.'

'And for the long haul.' He kissed her back.

CHAPTER SIXTEEN

Iris had been right. When Bugsy got to the station next day, he had a lump on his head the size of an egg, covered by a large dressing and a black eye that was all but closed.

'Flippin' heck, Sarge, what happened to you?' Aled peered at it with something akin to awe. 'I bet the other bloke looks worse.'

'There wasn't another bloke, young Aled. I don't go looking for a fight. It happened at home.'

Jack had overheard the saga of the inappropriate birthday gift when he'd interrupted the ladies' pitting cherries in the kitchen. He couldn't resist a comment. 'I remember Iris saying she threw the underwear at your head, but she didn't say she wrapped it round a brick first.'

Bugsy was aware of the giggles spreading around the office. 'I'm glad you all find this amusing. Before anyone starts ugly rumours about the state of my marriage, it was an accident. I tripped over the cat and bashed my head on the sink.'

Privately, Jack was thankful he hadn't got as far as giving Corrie the fluorescent yellow peephole bra and matching open crotch panties now that he knew how such items were perceived by ladies of a certain age. He suspected he'd have ended up in A&E with his head stuck in a blender. Mentally, he had written off the enormous expense that would have kept him in Y-fronts for a year, as he was too embarrassed to return the items and ask for a refund.

Clive was oblivious to what was going on around him, having made an interesting discovery from the satnav disc. Once it was dried out, he'd been able to track the last destination that had been programmed into it before the crash.

'Sir, you may want to take a look at this.'

The team gathered around his screen. Clive had managed to find the map clearly showing Bryn Thomas's route.

'Does that mean what I think it means?' asked Bugsy. 'Thomas programmed it to take him from his house in Kings Richington straight to the place known as Devil's Drop.'

'That's right, Sarge.'

'Why would he do that?' wondered Jack. 'Why didn't he put his hotel as his destination? It's what most people do, to be sure of finding it in the dark when it's late.'

'Despite what I said before, that kind of points to the actions of a man intending to kill himself,' said Gemma.

'But when we interviewed her, Felicity Thomas was adamant that he wouldn't do that. She said he had everything to live for,' Bugsy recalled.

Velma looked thoughtful. 'After a person has committed suicide, it's surprising how many of their friends and relatives say exactly that. They're often the last to know the state of mind of the deceased at the time he or she made the decision to end it all. They very often take themselves off somewhere to do it, where their loved ones won't be the first to discover their body. It's a last act of selflessness.'

'In that case,' said Jack briskly, 'that certainly wouldn't have applied to Bryn Thomas. Whatever traits he possessed, selflessness certainly wasn't one of them. I don't buy the suicide hypothesis. We need to look deeper. I'll ask Sergeant Parsloe to send uniforms to pick up Geoff Smart and Felicity Thomas in separate cars. We'll put them in two interview rooms and question them individually. I don't want them to confer on their phones — and that's important.'

* * *

Geoff Smart was clearly put out at being taken to the police station and placed in an interview room without any explanation. When Jack and Bugsy joined him, he was uncharacteristically truculent.

'Isn't this all a bit cloak-and-dagger, Inspector Dawes? Two uniformed police officers turn up at my garage and ask me to go with them without telling me why. Have I been arrested? If so, what for?'

'No, not at all, sir. We just needed another word with you without any interruptions.' *And without giving you the chance to phone Felicity Thomas and compare notes before we could speak to her.* 'We know you're a busy man.'

'So what is it you want to know that is so important it couldn't wait?' He noticed Bugsy's injuries. 'Goodness me, Sergeant, whatever happened to you?' He pointed to the lump and the black eye. 'I trust you arrested whoever did that.'

'It was just an accident at home, sir. We're here to ask you about the car you sold to Bryn Thomas.'

'I do hope you're not going to suggest there was anything wrong with it,' Smart protested. 'All my cars are thoroughly serviced and given a clean bill of health before I even put them on the forecourt, never mind sell them. I can assure you, that car was in perfect working order when I sold it to Thomas.'

'We don't doubt that, Mr Smart. Our police engineers have confirmed it.'

Jack watched him visibly relax and the car salesman's smile returned.

'So what is it I can help you with?'

Bugsy took over the questioning. 'It's about the satnav, sir.'

Jack watched him for a reaction. He believed he saw a slight flicker of apprehension, but he couldn't be sure.

'What about it?' asked Smart.

'Who programmed the destination in Wales that Mr Thomas was visiting for the music festival?'

'He did it himself, of course. I had no idea where he was going and I didn't ask. You have to understand, Inspector, you didn't have friendly chats with a man like Bryn. He had no social skills whatsoever. Most of the time he was bloody rude. If you challenged him on anything at all, however trivial, he took it as an attack on his manhood and the conversation descended into a metaphorical dick-measuring contest. He gave poor Fliss a terrible time.'

'Did you have any conversation with him at all?'

'No. I was busy with other customers. He just left his old car that I had agreed to try to sell, picked up the new one and drove off. The next I heard was that he had driven it off a cliff. I'm assuming he ignored the satnav because he thought he knew better. That was typical Bryn.'

There was a long pause, then Jack broke the silence. 'While you're here, sir, I wonder if you would clear up another matter concerning Charlie Snell.'

'Dear me, Inspector, am I to be questioned about every death on your caseload?'

'Not at all, but a member of the public overheard you having an altercation with him. Do you remember saying, "I know what you're up to, Snell, and you can pack it in or you'll be sorry"?'

'Yes, I do. The slimy bastard was trying to blackmail a friend of mine and I put a stop to it, but I didn't have to kill him to do it. Is that enough of an explanation for you?'

'For now, sir. There's just one last question and we'll let you get back to your work. What's your relationship with Mrs Thomas?'

He blinked at that one. 'If you mean a romantic relationship, as in a man-woman thing, we don't have one. I like to think I'm a good friend, though, and I shall help Fliss all I can, now that Bryn's gone. Practical help, such as finding her a reliable car.' He stood up. 'If that's everything, can I go now?'

'Yes, of course, sir. I'll get a police officer to drive you back.'

* * *

Felicity Thomas was in a room down the corridor, out of earshot of the interview with Smart. She was very nervous at being in a police station for all sorts of reasons. By the time Jack and Bugsy came in, she was almost hyperventilating. 'Why am I here, Inspector? I'm supposed to be arranging Bryn's funeral. It's most inconvenient.'

'We won't keep you long, Madam,' Bugsy assured her. 'Just a few loose ends we need to tie up.'

She stared at his head. 'Dear me, Sergeant, whatever happened to . . .?'

'Just an accident, Madam.' Bugsy cut her off, fed up with explaining and wanting to get straight to the matter in hand. Do you know if your late husband's new car had satnav fitted?'

'What? No. I don't know. It might have; I didn't see it. Bryn picked it up from Geoff's garage and drove straight off.' She gave a hollow laugh. 'Even if it did have satnav, it wouldn't have been any use to him.'

'Why is that?' asked Jack cautiously.

'Well, he wouldn't have known how to work it, would he? What I mean is, he understood music, but he was hopeless at anything technical. I even had to show him how to text people on his smartphone. And as for paying parking charges on a website, you wouldn't believe the number of penalty notices he got. He was a technophobe, although he would never admit it.'

'That's very interesting,' said Jack. 'Do you know the name of the place where the music festival was being held?'

'Not off the top of my head. It had a Welsh name, obviously. I know it began with *Aber* but then so do a lot of Welsh place names, don't they?'

'Had your husband been there before?'

'Not since he was very young. He said he was looking forward to seeing North Wales again. He never did like Kings Richington, and once the choir was disbanded, there was nothing to stop him going to the festival.'

'How was he proposing to find his way there?'

'I've absolutely no idea. He certainly couldn't read a map. And anyway, Bryn wasn't the kind of man you asked those sorts of questions, so I didn't.'

'Did he have a good sense of direction?'

'No. He was hopeless. He could get lost in an empty room.'

'One last question. What is your relationship with Mr Smart?'

She blushed slightly. 'He's a very good friend. He's been kind and looked after me when times were . . . difficult.'

'Well, thank you for being so frank, Mrs Thomas. I'll get someone to drive you home.'

* * *

'Right, team.' Jack stood in front of the whiteboard with the whole of MIT paying rapt attention. 'We have two totally opposite accounts of Bryn Thomas's ability to find his way to Aberfechan using satnav. Geoff Smart claims he knew how to programme it and did so himself. His wife, Felicity Thomas, says he didn't have a clue and couldn't find his bum with both hands and the light on. Who do we believe?'

'Definitely the wife, sir,' shouted someone at the back.

'Why?' asked Jack.

'Because he'd been married to her for some years and she'd be the best person to know.'

'I agree,' shouted someone else.

'So that means Geoff Smart was lying,' said Jack. 'Clive, our resident techno-genius, says the satnav had been set to take Thomas straight to Devil's Drop and, as we now know, over the edge.'

'I think they were in cahoots,' said Trevor, the young man who monitored and distributed the emails.

'Cahoots — is that an official term, Trevor?' asked Jack, amused.

'I watch a lot of Westerns, sir. I think Smart and Mrs Thomas are in a relationship and plotted to kill Mr Thomas to get him out of their way.'

'That would seem the most logical explanation, I agree. Although it would have carried more credibility if they'd collaborated beforehand and told the same story.'

'But . . .' interrupted Aled, 'if Smart purposely set the satnav to take Thomas over the edge, how could he be sure he'd follow it? I mean, you'd have to be daft to just blindly keep going even when it looked dodgy.'

'People do,' said Gemma. 'There are cases of drivers ending up in all sorts of weird places by religiously following their satnav.'

'It was because Smart told him to,' declared Velma loftily. 'The power of suggestion is much stronger than most people realize. If I were a betting person, I'd put my money on Smart telling Thomas he'd get hopelessly lost if he didn't follow the satnav to the letter. Late at night, in a howling storm, getting lost would have been the last thing he wanted.'

'What's the power of suggestion, Velma?' asked Aled.

'Suggestion,' she explained, 'is a psychological process by which someone can influence another person's behaviour by stimulating their reflexes, instead of conscious effort. In other words, when an idea is conveyed to them convincingly enough, that idea becomes reality and bypasses common sense.'

'Thank you,' he muttered under his breath. *I wish I hadn't asked now.*

'From a crime perspective,' said Gemma, whose law degree underpinned most of her thinking, 'it raises an interesting dilemma. If Smart did purposely set Thomas's satnav in the hopes of killing him — and we only have his word that he didn't — how would we prove it?'

'The short answer is — we couldn't,' Jack maintained. 'And I'm not even sure what we could charge him with. "Attempted murder" would be laughed out of court by an even halfway competent lawyer, and that's assuming the CPS accepted it, which is doubtful.'

'So unless one of them cracks, guv, we're left with a coroner's verdict of accidental death — or even death by misadventure, where the deceased took a deliberate action that resulted in his death.' Bugsy finished the last of Iris's jam tarts and wiped his fingers on his tie.

'Correct, Sergeant. Looks like this is going to be the one that got away.'

'Make that two, sir,' said Aled. 'We still haven't caught whoever killed Charlie Snell.'

Jack frowned. 'So the Chief Super keeps reminding me.'

* * *

'This time next week, my darling, we'll be in the Caribbean sipping rum punch out of pineapple halves.' Geoff poured Fliss another glass of champagne.

They were curled up on the hearth rug in front of the fire where logs crackled in the Edwardian arched fireplace. Heavy maroon velvet curtains covered sky-high windows, keeping out the draughts.

'It's going to be wonderful. I can hardly wait.' Fliss put her head on his shoulder. 'Are you sure we're in the clear now?'

'Yes, of course. Why wouldn't we be? That Inspector Dawes is a clever copper, but he can't pin anything on us. Trust me.'

'Oh, I do, Geoff.' She sipped her champagne thoughtfully. 'What would we have done if Bryn hadn't driven over the cliff?'

'I'd have found another way. He had to die, otherwise how would you have got this house back and control of your money?'

'I know. Is it wrong of me to feel as if a huge weight has been lifted?'

'Not at all. The man was impossible. You couldn't reason with him. He had to be crushed, like an irritating insect. There was no other way to set you free.'

'What about the other business?' She looked up at him, her eyes big, blue and trusting, and Geoff realized she was completely smitten.

'Don't think about that. It's all in the past. Just concentrate on the future, my darling.'

CHAPTER SEVENTEEN

Two months later

The whiteboard in the MIT incident room still stubbornly displayed every detail they had on Charlie Snell's murder except for the name of the murderer. There was an enlarged image of his body, lying in a clearing in Richington Forest, bashed over the head with a tree branch. Alongside were the names of everyone who might have had a motive, crossed through when they were investigated and no longer suspects. A photo of the shabby butcher's shop in which Mrs Snell was still working was a dismal memorial to an even more dismal life.

Similarly, there was still a question mark over the death of Bryn Thomas, although it had been officially recorded as misadventure. Aled had enlarged the photograph of each corpse to concentrate their minds on finding a solution, before both deaths disappeared into the graveyard of cold, unsolved cases. The silence was broken by Bugsy's phone. It was Sergeant Parsloe.

'Bugsy, I've got someone on the desk who says he's come to see the MIT.'

'Well, send him up, Norman. We could do with a distraction. It's like Brighton Beach on a wet Wednesday up here.'

'I would do, Bugsy, but the young man's on crutches and the lift's broken, until the engineers decide to turn up. Could you send someone down to help him, only I shouldn't leave the desk unattended.'

'No problem. I'll send young Aled. He's a big strong lad.' He put down the phone and called across. 'Aled, son, despite our strict adherence to the very complicated PACE accessibility rules, it doesn't cover getting someone on crutches upstairs when the lift's knackered. Can you go down and give "them" a hand?' He nudged Gemma. 'See what I did there, DC Fox? Gender-neutral pronoun.'

'I'm proud of you, Sarge.' She grinned. 'I don't listen to the people who call you a reactionary relic.'

'Thanks, Gemma.' He did a double take. 'What people?'

She was saved from a response when the door opened and Aled appeared, supporting a beaming DC 'Chippy' Chippendale. Everyone crowded around, shaking his hand and hugging him gingerly. Such was his popularity within the team that Jack could see the genuine delight that he was back amongst them, even though he was on crutches.

Bugsy fetched him a chair. 'DC Chippendale, it's good to see you. How are you feeling?'

'Pretty good, Sarge, thanks. The medics say I'll soon be fighting fit again. No long-term injuries.'

DC Fox gave him a rare kiss. 'I suppose you'll be off back to New Zealand as soon as you're able to travel.'

Chippy's face fell. 'What? No. I'm coming back here to do my job. Aren't I, sir?' He looked at Jack for confirmation. 'I haven't been fired, have I? I know what I did was daft, but I shan't do it again. I've learned my lesson.'

'Chippy, mate, the last we heard was that your mum was taking you back home to be a flautist,' Aled told him.

'She means well, bless her. She's a Professor of Musicology at Auckland University. But there's no way I'm going back.' Chippy was adamant. 'For a start, my jaw has been reconstructed and I've had new front teeth implanted.

I doubt I could even play the flute now, even if I wanted to.' He looked forlorn. 'I can come back, can't I, Inspector?'

'Of course, Detective Constable. Any time you're ready and the doctors pronounce you fit.' Jack called out, 'Someone fetch Chippy a coffee to celebrate.'

While he waited, Chippy hobbled to the whiteboard to see what progress had been made since he was last there. He'd been following developments closely from reports in the *Richington Echo*, but he didn't believe everything the press put out. He'd kept up with the accounts of Dr Amory, charged with the murders of Luke Burton and Violet Dibble, and read about the choirmaster, Bryn Thomas, driving his car off a cliff. With any luck, he reckoned he'd be back working on the cases as soon as he passed the fitness test. He stared at the two enlarged photographs then asked Aled, 'Is that the same bloke — Charlie Snell?'

'No.' Aled pointed. 'That's Charlie Snell. The other one's Bryn Thomas. The Charlie Snell murder is proving particularly difficult to crack. Apart from him being an all-round crook, blackmailer and a nasty piece of work, we haven't established the exact motive or a stand-out suspect for his murder.'

Chippy thought about it for a bit. 'What if there isn't one?'

'What d'you mean, son?' asked Bugsy. 'There must have been a clear-cut motive that drove someone to kill him.'

'Not necessarily, Sarge. What if it was a simple case of mistaken identity?' He hobbled closer and pointed. 'Both men were similar builds, tall and slim, wore their hair in a ponytail and had beards. Charlie Snell is wearing a jacket with a Welsh dragon logo on the back; he probably nicked it from Bryn in the pub one night when it was raining. In these photos, taken from behind, they look very similar. Identical even — if you're stumbling about in the dark, in a forest, in the rain. If I got them mixed up, what if the murderer did, too?'

'You mean the murderer thought he'd killed Bryn Thomas?' said Jack.

'They,' corrected Bugsy. 'Gender-neutral pronoun, guv. We don't know the murderer was a bloke, do we? Big Ron said it could just as easily have been a woman, or even both. Joint enterprise, maybe.'

'Geoff Smart and Felicity Thomas,' proclaimed Velma. 'They got it wrong the first time, so had another go with the satnav. If that hadn't worked, I'm pretty sure they would have tried again.'

'Chippy, you might just have something there,' said Jack. 'It was staring us in the face, but we'd been looking at it for too long. It needed a fresh pair of eyes. We're looking forward to you coming back.'

* * *

'Oh Geoff, Barbados is wonderful. I wish we could stay here forever.' Felicity was soaking up the sun and the breathtaking view from the private villa they had occupied for the last four weeks. They had snorkelled among the shimmering reefs, danced the night away to salsa rhythms and walked on the sugar-sand beaches. 'I love everything about it — the weather, the beautiful turquoise sea and the nightlife.' She looked at him coyly from beneath her lashes. 'It's the perfect place for a honeymoon, wouldn't you say? We are getting married, aren't we?'

'Of course we are, sweetheart. Once everything has settled down and the police have given up investigating us for good.'

She was thoughtful. 'We don't have to live in Kings Richington, though, do we? Such bad memories.'

'But would you be happy to sell your house?' Geoff asked. 'You've lived there all your life.'

'Oh yes. The years I've lived there with Bryn have cast a dark, oppressive shadow over it. It doesn't feel safe anymore. Then there was that awful Charlie Snell, trying to get money out of me because he'd caught you and me kissing after choir practice.'

'He needed to be taught a lesson. There were no depths that bloke wouldn't sink to. His murder might have been a mistake, sweetheart, but in the end, it put a stop to his blackmail racket and probably reassured a lot of people. You could consider it an act of public service.'

'Philanthropic, in fact.' She laughed.

'I doubt if Inspector Dawes would see it like that. He's not a bad bloke — for a copper. Just not very quick on the uptake.'

Felicity was thinking. 'What will we do about your garage, Geoff?'

'It'll be easy enough to sell. It's a going concern with a good reputation.'

'Unless you're a customer looking for a car with a satnav that won't take you over a cliff,' said Felicity. They laughed.

'I can't believe the police fell for that,' said Felicity. 'They're not very clever, are they?'

'Not as clever as us, my darling.' Geoff stood up. 'Let's go for one last swim and a cocktail, before we go home.'

'I wish we didn't have to.' Felicity was downcast at the thought.

'Chin up, sweetheart. We'll go home, sort out the practical stuff, then come back here while we decide where we're going to spend the rest of our lives.'

* * *

'Do we know where Geoff Smart and Felicity Thomas have gone?' Jack asked the team. Checks with the neighbours of the Edwardian house and Smart's Autos had revealed that they were on holiday, but nobody knew where.

'Well, I don't expect they're in a boarding house in Southend,' commented Clive. 'I've checked Felicity Thomas's financial situation and she has regained control of her money, which is considerable. And her solicitor has had the house put back in her name. My guess is that they've gone somewhere exotic and expensive. Smart's deputy manager at the garage told us what day they left. I'll check the passenger lists at the airports, sir.' Two hours later, he had discovered where they had gone. 'They're in Barbados, sir, but they're coming back. Their return flight is the day after tomorrow. And the magistrate has issued that warrant that you asked for.'

'Well done, Clive. We'll have a welcome party waiting to bring them in. This time, we'll question them about the Snell murder.'

* * *

Heathrow Airport was heaving when Geoff and Felicity's plane touched down. When they reached Customs, there were two uniformed police officers waiting for them and a police car outside. Geoff took Felicity's arm and muttered, 'Don't panic, Fliss. It'll just be some routine matter that they need us to clear up. If they'd had anything substantial, they'd have arrested us before we left.'

Once again, they were taken to the station in separate cars and put into separate interview rooms. Jack and Bugsy decided to question Smart first. He was the truculent, bolshy one while Felicity Thomas looked scared to death and declared she felt faint. The custody sergeant got her a glass of water and left her to calm down.

Velma was operating the recording machine this time and performed the usual preliminaries.

'What do you want this time, Inspector?' Smart demanded. 'This is getting perilously close to harassment. Should I call my solicitor?'

'Do you think you need one, sir?' asked Jack. 'You haven't been charged with anything — yet.'

'So what's it all about, then? Mrs Thomas and I have just come back from a relaxing holiday to find your officers lying in wait for us, as if we were common criminals. I've told you everything I know about Bryn Thomas's unfortunate accident and so has Mrs Thomas. The coroner's verdict was misadventure. I fail to see what more . . .'

'It isn't Bryn Thomas we want to talk to you about, sir,' said Bugsy. 'It's Charlie Snell.'

'Good God, man, Snell had more scams going than Al Capone. If you're looking for someone who wanted him dead, stick a pin in the Kings Richington telephone directory.'

'We're following a different line of enquiry from Snell's enemies, sir.' Jack watched his face, as did Velma. 'We think it's possible that he was murdered by someone who had mistaken him for Bryn Thomas.'

Smart was silent for long moments. 'That's preposterous,' he said finally. 'Why have you got it into your heads that someone wanted to murder Bryn? The man was an insufferable narcissist and he treated poor Fliss appallingly, but I can't think of anyone who'd want to kill him.'

'What about you and Mrs Thomas?' asked Jack. 'It suited your purpose to have him out of the way, didn't it? If you or Mrs Thomas had come upon him — or thought you had — in the forest on that dark and stormy night after choir practice, you might have been tempted to get him out of your lives once and for all.'

Bugsy kept up the pressure. 'When it turned out you'd killed the wrong man, you had to think of another way.'

Smart stood up. 'I'm not listening to another word of this. If I'm not under arrest, I'm leaving and I'm taking Fliss with me.'

'As you wish, sir. You can go, but I'm afraid we need to question Mrs Thomas before she can be released.'

'Now look, Dawes, you go easy on her. Fliss is fragile. She doesn't know anything about Snell's death. She was at home with Bryn when Snell was murdered. She has an alibi.'

'That's just it, Mr Smart.' Jack stood up then and faced him. 'She doesn't have an alibi. The last time we spoke with Mr Thomas, he admitted that he lied about going straight home after choir practice. He went to Richington Forest to meet Snell, intending to thrash him because he was demanding money to keep quiet about Bryn's time in prison. But when he got there, he found him dead. Bryn then called in at the pub for a drink to steady himself before going home. That means Mrs Thomas doesn't have an alibi for all that time.'

'You can't prove a thing.' His chin jutted out belligerently.

'Well, you see, this is why we need to question Mrs Thomas. The forensic officers took casts of all the footprints at the crime scene. Apart from Snell's own prints and Dr Amory's, who found the body, and Bryn's tracks on the edge of the clearing, there's another set of smallish ones that belong to the killer. All we need to do is see if we can match them to Mrs Thomas.' Jack stood aside to let Smart pass, but he didn't move. 'While you were on holiday, I obtained a warrant to enter Mrs Thomas's house and impound all her shoes. We've also taken possession of the ones in her suitcase. It shouldn't take long for the lab to do a comparison.'

Velma had been watching Smart throughout. He was bearing down on the inspector, showing all the signs of uncontrolled rage, even Oppositional Defiant Disorder, the urge to thwart and defeat anyone in a role of authority. She had seen it explode into violence on several occasions and was thankful for the constable by the door and another outside.

Eventually, Smart sat down again. 'All right, Dawes, you win. I confess. I did it — I killed Snell. Fliss had nothing to do with it. Now, leave her alone.'

'But you didn't, did you, Mr Smart?' Bugsy, the other half of the interrogation tag team, took over. 'You couldn't have killed Snell, because we've got clear footage of you on CCTV, leaving the Richington Arms that night, driving to your garage and going in to do some paperwork. You didn't leave until well after the murder was committed and you didn't go anywhere near the forest.'

That lit the touchpaper, and as Velma expected, the firework exploded. Smart almost roared his frustration and swung a punch which, had it landed, would have given Bugsy a lump on the other side of his head. Instead, the constable on the door, trained to sense a fracas, leapt forward and grabbed Smart's arm. The officer outside burst through the door and grabbed Smart's other arm, and together they frog-marched him outside and down to the cells to cool off.

'Blimey, that was close,' remarked Bugsy.

'Don't worry, Sergeant, we'll speak to Felicity Thomas now,' decided Jack. 'I don't expect she punches her weight.'

* * *

The police officer had brought Felicity a cup of tea, but she was too nervous to drink it. She felt sick, wondering what was happening to Geoff. He'd told her to say nothing, but she couldn't just sit there in silence. She'd never been in trouble with the police in her whole life, not even a parking ticket. She wondered where the solicitor was that she'd been promised. Right on cue, the door opened and Jack and Bugsy came in, followed by Gemma to operate the recording and the duty solicitor. She was so on edge she jumped almost out of her skin and knocked over her tea.

They went through the necessary introductions for the tape, then Jack began. 'Mrs Thomas, I need to ask you where you were between ten thirty and eleven thirty on . . .' He looked down at his notes and read out the date . . . when Charlie Snell was murdered.

'Er . . .' She swallowed hard. 'I don't remember. I've been out of the country since then. I can't remember much of anything before that. It's the trauma of my husband dying so unexpectedly. I'm sorry.'

'Perhaps this will jog your memory.' Jack opened his file, took out a photograph of Snell's dead body and pushed it across the desk towards her.

She recoiled and pushed it back. 'I remember where I was now. Bryn and I had been to choir practice. We went straight home, had a late supper and went to bed. Yes, that's it.'

'No, that isn't it, Mrs Thomas.' Bugsy took up the questioning. 'Before he died, your late husband changed his statement. After the choir practice, he said he came home with you, then he went out again and so did you. He went to the place in Richington Forest where he had arranged to meet Snell and found him dead, bludgeoned with an oak branch. Where did you go?'

'Oh yes, I remember now. I went for a walk.'

There was a tap on the door. It opened and Aled put his head round. 'Sarge, can I have a word?'

Bugsy left the room and Gemma mentioned it for the benefit of the tape. When he came back in, Bugsy was holding two photo enlargements. He slid them in front of Jack, then he sat down again. Jack studied them for some moments then he put one in front of Felicity.

'This is a photograph of a footprint we found at the crime scene. We are confident it belongs to the murderer. While you were on holiday, forensic officers compared it to the soles of all your shoes.' He pushed the second sheet in front of her. 'We found a perfect match to the cleats on this trainer. Do you recognize it?'

She burst into tears and buried her face in her hands. 'I didn't mean to kill him. It was a terrible mistake. I thought it was Bryn — it looked exactly like him from behind.'

'Let's get this right, Mrs Thomas,' said Jack. 'Your late husband went out and you followed him.'

She looked at her solicitor and he nodded. 'Yes. He wouldn't tell me where he was going and I wanted to see what he was up to. I thought he'd found out about Geoff and me and he was going to hurt him. I saw Bryn on the path going into the forest and I followed him. It was a terrible night, gusts of wind and heavy rain, and for a while, I lost sight of him. I blundered around for a bit then I thought I spotted him, standing in a clearing. That was my chance to rid myself of a self-serving, obnoxious bully who made my life a misery. I picked up the branch, crept up behind him and hit him, hard. Then I ran home.'

'What did you think had happened when your husband, who you believed you'd killed, suddenly walked in unharmed?' Bugsy thought it must have been a defining moment.

'I was shocked — horrified. Then, next day, when everyone was talking about Charlie being found dead in a clearing in the forest, I realized what had happened. It was awful. If it hadn't been for Geoff, I don't know what I'd have done.'

Jack pushed back his chair. 'Mrs Thomas, will you stand up, please?'

She stood up, confused, and looked desperately towards her solicitor for help. He didn't return her gaze but looked down at his notes, then closed the file.

'Mrs Thomas,' Jack intoned, 'I'm charging you with the murder of Charlie Snell . . . you do not have to say anything but . . .'

'No,' she wept. 'It wasn't murder. How could it be? It was a mistake. I didn't mean to kill Charlie.'

'Maybe not, but you did mean to kill your husband. You're being charged with murder for killing your *unintended* victim because his death occurred during your commission of the crime of attempted murder of your *intended* victim. To put it simply, trying to kill someone and just being an incompetent murderer is no defence.' He finished the caution and the uniformed officers took her down, sobbing.

CHAPTER EIGHTEEN

'Fancy Felicity Thomas killing Charlie Snell in mistake for Bryn. Who'd have believed it?' Corrie was taking canapés out of the oven and putting them on a tray to cool. 'She's such a mousey little thing, unassuming and harmless. Or so we all thought.' She cautioned Jack, who had pinched a profiterole filled with melted camembert. 'Don't put that straight in your mouth, it's—'

It was too late and Jack huffed and puffed and took a gulp of chilled Sauvignon Blanc. 'Why do you have to make them so bloomin' hot?' He swished the wine around his mouth in an attempt to deaden the pain.

'It's called cooking, Jack. You put stuff in the oven — it comes out hot. Deal with it.' She pondered. 'I don't think any of us guessed Felicity was having an affair with Geoff Smart. We all thought he was seeing Roxy Wild.'

'I think that's what he wanted people to think. It took the focus off Felicity and stopped Bryn getting suspicious.' He took another canapé, and this time, he pulled it in half and blew on the molten cheese. 'Considering you weren't in the choir, you seem to know a lot of the inside gossip about the members.'

'It's because we live in a vibrant community, Jack. You only have to look at all the lovely activities that take place in our Community Hall — Arts and Crafts, Coffee and Crochet Mornings, WI Meetings, Film Clubs, Mothers and Toddlers, Tea Dances for the Elderly and, of course, the choir practices. The list is endless. It's a veritable treasure trove of worthy community programmes.'

'How many of those do you go to?' asked Jack.

'Well, I don't, obviously, but my point is that I could if I wanted to.' She poured herself a glass of wine before Jack used it all as mouthwash. 'The downside, of course, is that a community, by definition, is also a hotbed of scandal and intrigue. Before it collapsed under the weight of its own depravity, the Richington Community Choir was the perfect cover for those folk who thrive on salacious gossip and those with a desire for power and control. Elizabeth Amory is an obvious example. In between the songs, they learned people's weaknesses and gained information about the other members that they could use against them later. That's what communities are all about. You keep tabs on everyone, find out everything about their lives, and if possible, you make money out of it. For example, Charlie Snell — master of dirty tricks and dodgy deals.'

'You make it sound like a den of iniquity instead of a group of people getting together for a jolly singalong.'

'Well, look at it this way — you have four murders, two choir members awaiting sentence and a detective constable beaten up so badly he could have died, and all connected in some way to the activities of the choir. And that doesn't include blackmail, adultery, fraud and a fake passport scam. Does that sound like a jolly singalong to you?'

'Well, no, not if you put it like that . . .'

'I do. And before I forget, don't plan anything for Saturday evening. We've been invited out to a posh dinner party at Chez Carlene.'

Jack groaned. 'Not Saturday, it's the rugby play-off.'

'Well, record it, sweetheart.'

'It isn't the same. Someone always puts the highlights on TV and social media before I've had a chance to watch it.

Couldn't you go and give them my apologies? Tell whoever it is that I had an important meeting?'

'What? On a Saturday night? I don't think so, and anyway, we have to go; it would be rude not to. Aubrey and Alicia Chippendale are hosting a night out for the whole team, even George and Cynthia, to thank us for rescuing Chippy after he was attacked. They're going back to New Zealand at the beginning of the week, so it has to be Saturday.'

'Professor Chippendale doesn't still think she's taking Chippy with her, does she? Only he made it clear to me that he wants to stay with the team.'

'No. I think she realizes that although he still looks like her little boy, he's his own man and can choose what he wants to do in life and that isn't playing the flute. Mind you, it would probably be safer.'

'I'm not so sure,' said Jack. 'How do you know orchestras aren't as toxic as community choirs?'

* * *

The whiteboard was, at last, mercifully clear now that Felicity Thomas had been arrested and charged with the outstanding murder of Charlie Snell. She was able to pay for an expensive defence lawyer, so whilst there was no doubt that she had wilfully put an end to a life, there was still a lot of debate with the CPS as to the exact charges. As for Geoff Smart, they were still scratching their heads trying to decide if he had even committed a classifiable crime.

'What do you reckon, sir?' asked Aled. 'Given the circumstances and Felicity Thomas's insistence that Bryn couldn't programme an egg-timer, it's almost certain that Geoff Smart set the satnav with the hope and intention that Thomas would drive off the cliff.'

'Yes, but what recognizable crime did he actually commit?' persisted Gemma. 'For a start, there are no witnesses to prove that it was Smart and not Thomas who programmed it. And Bryn Thomas didn't have to blindly follow the satnav just because Smart told him to. He had eyes; he could have got out of the car, looked where he was going, bought a map or asked directions, but he didn't. I think any prosecuting counsel could have a problem.'

'Fortunately, it's their problem and not ours,' declared Jack. 'We've put all the evidence before the Crown Prosecutors and they will decide if they have a strong enough case to proceed.'

'So can we finally draw a line under the Richington Choir Killer, sir?' asked Aled.

'Yes, but the irony is — there wasn't one.' Jack leaned back in his chair. 'There was no serial killer with a pathological dislike of choirs, picking them off at random, even though the editor of the *Echo* wanted readers to believe that. It lent his ongoing articles an air of intrigue and mystery. The truth was that the individuals who died were murdered for the usual mundane reason — that somebody wanted them out of the way.'

'That's right, guv,' agreed Bugsy. 'Young Luke Burton had to die because Elizabeth Amory believed his revelations would have ruined her standing in the community and scotched her lofty aspirations. Then after that, Mrs Dibble had to go because she could have destroyed Amory's alibi.'

Gemma took up the narrative. 'Charlie Snell's murder might have been a mistake, but I reckon there were a lot of folk in Richington who weren't sorry when they heard, and that includes his wife and son.'

'And the death of Bryn Thomas won't have left much of a gap in the choral community,' observed Velma. 'From what I can see, the only person who thought the Maestro was a musical genius was Bryn himself.'

Clive nodded. 'There are no fulsome obituaries on the choir sites, not even in his hometown.'

'On a more cheerful note,' announced Jack, 'don't forget the dinner party that Chippy's parents are hosting on Saturday night at Chez Carlene. All are invited. And even more good news — he's passed the fitness test and he'll be back on light duties on Monday.'

* * *

The bistro was buzzing. Carlene, Antoine and the staff were kept busy ensuring the Chippendales were happy with the food, drinks and service for which they had paid generously.

Chippy, overjoyed to be back amongst his colleagues again, stood up and tapped his glass. The room erupted with cries of 'speech'.

'Thank you all for coming and thanks to my folks for putting on a *beaut* night out.' The amount of champagne he'd drunk caused him to slip into his native New Zealand. 'But none of this could have happened, and I wouldn't even be here, if it hadn't been for Corrie, the DI's missus, and Carlene, owner of this very posh caff.' He pointed towards them, sitting together in an alcove. 'You guys are bloody legends.' He continued, 'When those two ladies rescued me from the bad bastards, I thought I'd carked it and two angels had come to take me to heaven — or maybe the other place.' There was laughter. 'I can't describe the journey except to say it felt like racing round Silverstone in the back of a chuck wagon with Lewis Hamilton at the wheel. I don't remember much until I woke up in hospital, but trust me, you don't want to get on the wrong side of Carlene when she has a frying pan in her hand, eh?' More laughter. He looked directly at Jack. 'Thank you, sir, for taking me back into the MIT and I promise I won't let you down again.' He sat down to raucous cheers and clapping.

'Bless him,' said Carlene. 'Aren't you glad we stopped and picked him up, Mrs D?'

Corrie nodded. 'His mum came and spoke to me earlier. Obviously, she loves all her children, but I got the feeling Chippy is her favourite. She still isn't happy about him staying here in Kings Richington, but she accepts it's what he wants and she said she was glad he had such good friends and colleagues to support him.'

'Sensible woman.' Carlene was silent for a while. 'You know, Mrs D, I still can't get my head around Elizabeth Amory sticking a knife into her own son. What kind of woman does that?'

'An evil one,' said Corrie shortly. 'What really scares me is if she'd got as far as standing for mayor, I'd probably have voted for her. She seemed so committed to serving the community.'

'Yeah, but at any cost, even murder,' concluded Carlene. 'That's where it went tits up.'

* * *

George and Cynthia Garwood were relaxing in a window seat, enjoying the proceedings. George was especially relaxed now that the crime reports had gone up the line to Sir Barnaby showing a total clear-up. He'd gone so far as to help himself to his favourite devilled eggs, although they were renowned for giving him indigestion.

'It's a good turnout,' he remarked, looking around at the MIT folk and their partners enjoying the party. 'The MIT has developed into a highly successful team under my leadership.'

Cynthia took another glass of champagne from the tray that the waiter was offering. 'Don't you mean under Jack's leadership? And while we're on the subject, he's been a detective inspector for a few years now. Don't you think it's time you recommended him for promotion?'

Such was George's affront at the suggestion that the stuffing in the egg he was holding trembled and hurled itself out onto his trousers. 'Oh no, Cynthia, I don't think so! He isn't ready.'

'Why isn't he? Didn't you say the NCA had commended his involvement in smashing the local passport racket and he's certainly caught a lot of bad guys over the years. Look how he put away the sons of that billionaire drugs and arms dealer. That must have been a huge feather in his cap.'

'Yes, but you only see the flamboyant, ostentatious side of Dawes' policing,' complained George. 'Like a lot of others, you're just impressed by the end results where he makes arrests and puts murderers in prison.'

'But isn't that exactly what he's supposed to do?' asked Cynthia.

'Yes, but he won't just leave it at that.' Garwood was getting petulant. 'The man's a loose cannon. He storms in like some flashy TV detective, cuts corners and flagrantly ignores PACE when it suits him. You wouldn't believe the number of times I've tried to impress upon him that resorting to the "Ways and Means Act" simply won't cut it. No, I couldn't possibly put him forward for Chief Inspector. It would reflect badly on my judgement.'

But if he were honest, Garwood knew his main objection was that Dawes made him feel intellectually inferior. He couldn't put his finger on the reason; it was insidious. There was nothing blatant that would enable him to issue an official reprimand; it was just an uncomfortable feeling he had. Ideally, he'd like to have the blasted man transferred to another division, but he knew what would happen. The clear-up results of Dawes' new division would skyrocket while his, Garwood's, would disappear into the 'need to improve' category. He had no illusions that the success of MIT was down to Dawes, but he didn't have to like it.

* * *

Jack and Corrie got home at three o'clock. Corrie had insisted on staying to help Carlene clear up, but now she was more than ready for bed. She had a quick shower then put on her Winnie-the-Pooh pyjamas and crept quietly into the bedroom in case Jack was already asleep. He was wide awake and sitting up in bed with a mug of hot chocolate laced with cognac. He'd turned on the wide-screen TV, fixed to the wall opposite the bed, and was scrolling through the recorded programmes.

'What are you doing?' protested Corrie. 'It's three thirty in the morning.'

'I'm going to watch the rugby. If I see it now, I won't be caught off guard by the result on the breakfast news in the morning, before I've had a chance to watch it.'

Corrie plumped up her pillow. 'Oh, I can tell you the results now, to save us both having to stay awake half the night. It was on the news channel on my phone. The final score was . . .'

'Nooooo!'

EPILOGUE

Jack and Bugsy were present at Dr Elizabeth Amory's trial when the jury found her guilty of the murders of Luke Burton and Violet Dibble. It was a unanimous decision. Given all the evidence and the assessments from external experts, the judge in the High Court decided he had enough information to pass sentence the same day and did not ask for further reports. His voice was booming and authoritative as he passed down two life sentences to run concurrently. She hadn't pleaded guilty to murder or shown remorse as she still maintained that what she'd done was what any reasonable person would have done under the same circumstances and that she'd had no choice. She was taken from the court and transported to a reception prison, pending relocation to a more secure unit, due to the severity of her crimes and the length of sentence.

Since neither Luke nor Violet had any known relatives, there was only Ellie Bishop in court to see that justice was done for her boyfriend. She was there in the public gallery, flanked by her parents, and shed tears as the sentence was read out. Luke had always told her she had a spectacular singing voice, and sad though she was, she resolved to carry on training in memory of his love for her.

Unknown to Jack and Bugsy, Aled had crept in at the back of the court towards the end of the proceedings and he applauded silently as Amory was taken away. Violet hadn't exactly been avenged, he thought, but at least her killer hadn't escaped retribution by claiming diminished responsibility or some other justification for which Velma could assign a politically correct name. As he left the court, he muttered, 'RIP, Violet,' and held three fingers to his forehead in her Girl Guide salute.

Outside the court, Bugsy was sombre. 'Amory looked sort of smaller than I recall, up there in the dock. Not so domineering and calculating — like when she believed she could take on the world without breaking step or observing decent rules like we mere mortals do.'

'It's worrying when you think that if we hadn't stopped her, she might easily have gone on to become Richington's mayor and maybe even our Member of Parliament. With her determination and utter ruthlessness, she could have ended up as Prime Minister.'

'Now that is a frightening thought,' said Bugsy. 'D'you fancy a pint, guv?'

* * *

Roxy Wild was scrolling through a dating website on her laptop while drowning her sorrows in Cabernet Sauvignon. *You're a silly woman*, she remonstrated with herself. *Geoff Smart used you to put Bryn Thomas and the Old Bill off the scent of his affair with Felicity. And there you were, thinking that an occasional shag meant he was seriously interested. How stupid was that?* She poured another glass. It wasn't as if she hadn't had experience of inadequate men. She'd been married and divorced twice, and both times, it had ended acrimoniously. And she ran a sex shop, for goodness' sake! If that didn't give you an insight into men's proclivities, she didn't know what did. She really should have known better. Now here she was, intending to sign up online for what she fully expected would be a dispiriting encounter with some old loser looking for sex, because his blow-up girlfriend had a puncture.

She hadn't heard what had happened to Geoff after Felicity Thomas had been sent to prison. She hadn't made any effort to find out, so she didn't know if he was still in police custody. The community rumour mill said that the police believed Geoff had tampered with Bryn's car in some way and that was why he'd driven off the cliff. She didn't believe it. Geoff was too shrewd for something so obvious and traceable. All the same, she was sure he'd had a hand in it somewhere.

The questions on the dating profile seemed to get sillier the more wine she drank. *Do you have a good sense of direction?* She'd once got lost in IKEA for two hours but decided that didn't count. She looked at some of the answers men had given when registering their profile. *How would you describe yourself in three words?* The bloke, whose picture had clearly been photoshopped to look like an embalmed Tom Cruise, had answered: *Youthful, confident and sensitive.* Roxy translated that to mean: *immature, self-absorbed and whiny.*

Why, she asked herself after two weary hours, *are you even doing this? Who needs a man, anyway?* She took herself off to bed with the rest of the Cabernet Sauvignon and the rabbit she had failed to sell to Bugsy.

* * *

Geoff Smart sold his garage and was planning to return to Barbados, since the police had not yet confiscated his passport. It seemed the authorities still couldn't decide if there was a crime they could charge him with that would stick in court. The last he'd heard, they were toying with gross negligence manslaughter. From what he could gather from his lawyer, it relied on the possible, but not proven, programming of Bryn's satnav in the car Smart had sold him. Was it reasonably foreseeable that it could give rise to a serious and obvious risk of death? And had it, in fact, caused death?

They couldn't decide if his conduct was enough to amount to a criminal act. He didn't believe they had a chance. Where was their evidence?

Whilst he had been in Barbados with Fliss, there had been an attractive and wealthy widow with a house in Kensington, holidaying in the next villa for the season. She had shown a polite interest in him, nodding, smiling and exchanging pleasantries, which he felt sure he could develop into something more meaningful. He could always spot the signs. It was clear that Fliss would be out of circulation for some years, having been given a lengthy stretch in prison for the murder of Charlie Snell. Her expensive KC had persuaded her that despite her denials as to intent, she should plead guilty, which had earned her a reduction in her sentence. Geoff had escaped an allegation of joint enterprise, because there was no proof that he positively intended that she should commit the murder and had neither assisted nor encouraged it. But all the same, he was aware that he wasn't getting any younger and who knew what was around the corner? He planned to get the next flight out to Barbados.

* * *

Jim Scuttle had been shocked when he heard what happened to DC Chippendale and felt somehow responsible, even though he couldn't have foreseen what had happened. One thing was certain — as long as he was landlord of the Richington Arms, young Chippy would always have drinks on the house. He resolved that in future, like Aled had suggested, if he suspected anything even slightly criminal was going on in his pub, he would report it to the police. Now that Jim was neither singing with the choir nor offering his upstairs room for practices, he felt strangely bereft, as singing did lift his spirits in a way that nothing else did. He knew several other ex-members of the choir had expressed a feeling of isolation now that there was no longer a get-together where they could meet up and sing. He wondered if he could form a new choir. How hard could it be? Bryn never seemed to do anything especially technical, although he never tired of telling everybody how lucky they were to have him as their Maestro. Well, Jim decided to give it a go. What did he have to lose? He'd go online, resurrect the blog and offer his upstairs room for the first meeting of the New Richington Choir.

* * *

A year later, the death of Bryn Thomas in the UK and Geoff Smart's suspected involvement in it had still not been resolved. Blithely unconcerned, Geoff was jet-skiing with his new lady friend on the sparkling azure sea surrounding the island of Barbados. It was an idyllic Caribbean day and they had planned a lunch of seafood in a beach-side restaurant afterwards. She was some distance behind him when she saw him suddenly fall off into the water. The jet ski engine cut and she waited for him to resurface, swim back and grab the reboarding handle to pull himself back up. It didn't happen. After a few moments, when he didn't reappear, she began to panic. Then she waved vigorously to the lifeguards on the beach.

The post-mortem came back with a ruptured brain aneurism as the cause of death. It had been instantaneous and there was nothing anyone could have done. When the report finally filtered through to the UK, the CPS closed the file but not before it had given Jack pause for thought. He wasn't a superstitious man. He didn't believe that black cats and walking under ladders brought you bad luck, but he couldn't help thinking that fate had taken a hand in bringing a fitting end to the ill-fortune that had plagued the Richington Community Choir.

THE END

THE JOFFE BOOKS STORY

We began in 2014 when Jasper agreed to publish his mum's much-rejected romance novel and it became a bestseller.

Since then we've grown into the largest independent publisher in the UK. We're extremely proud to publish some of the very best writers in the world, including Joy Ellis, Faith Martin, Caro Ramsay, Helen Forrester, Simon Brett and Robert Goddard. Everyone at Joffe Books loves reading and we never forget that it all begins with the magic of an author telling a story.

We are proud to publish talented first-time authors, as well as established writers whose books we love introducing to a new generation of readers.

We won Trade Publisher of the Year at the Independent Publishing Awards in 2023 and Best Publisher Award in 2024 at the People's Book Prize. We have been shortlisted for Independent Publisher of the Year at the British Book Awards for the last five years, and were shortlisted for the Diversity and Inclusivity Award at the 2022 Independent Publishing Awards. In 2023 we were shortlisted for Publisher of the Year at the RNA Industry Awards, and in 2024 we were shortlisted at the CWA Daggers for the Best Crime and Mystery Publisher.

We built this company with your help, and we love to hear from you, so please email us about absolutely anything bookish at feedback@joffebooks.com.

If you want to receive free books every Friday and hear about all our new releases, join our mailing list here: www.joffebooks.com/freebooks.

And when you tell your friends about us, just remember: it's pronounced Joffe as in coffee or toffee!